circ: 9
LAD: 9/2005

THE CAT
WHO TALKED
TURKEY

*Also by Lilian Jackson Braun
in Large Print:*

The Cat Who Ate Danish Modern
The Cat Who Lived High
The Cat Who Moved a Mountain
The Cat Who Came to Breakfast
The Cat Who Blew the Whistle
The Cat Who Said Cheese
The Cat Who Tailed a Thief
The Cat Who Robbed a Bank
The Cat Who Smelled a Rat
The Cat Who Went Up the Creek
The Cat Who Brought Down the House

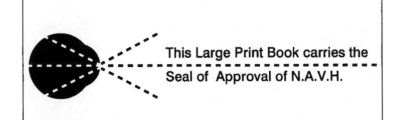

This Large Print Book carries the
Seal of Approval of N.A.V.H.

LILIAN JACKSON BRAUN

THE CAT WHO TALKED TURKEY

Thorndike Press • Waterville, Maine

Published in 2004 by arrangement with G. P. Putnam's Sons, a member of Penguin Group (USA) Inc.

Thorndike Press® Large Print Basic.

The tree indicium is a trademark of Thorndike Press.

The text of this Large Print edition is unabridged.
Other aspects of the book may vary from the original edition.

Set in 16 pt. Plantin by Liana M. Walker.

Printed in the United States on permanent paper.

Library of Congress Cataloging-in-Publication Data

Braun, Lilian Jackson.
    The cat who talked turkey / Lilian Jackson Braun.
      p. cm.
    ISBN 0-7862-6114-5 (lg. print : hc : alk. paper)
    1. Qwilleran, Jim (Fictitious character) — Fiction.
    2. Yum Yum (Fictitious character : Braun) — Fiction.
    3. Moose County (Imaginary place) — Fiction.
    4. Koko (Fictitious character) — Fiction. 5. Country life — Fiction. 6. Millionaires — Fiction. 7. Siamese cat — Fiction. 8. Journalists — Fiction. 9. Cat owners — Fiction. 10. Cats — Fiction. 11. Large type books. I. Title.
PS3552.R354C367 2004b
  813'.54—dc22   2003066314

Dedicated to Earl Bettinger,
The Husband Who . . .

As the Founder/CEO of NAVH, the only national health agency solely devoted to those who, although not totally blind, have an eye disease which could lead to serious visual impairment, I am pleased to recognize Thorndike Press* as one of the leading publishers in the large print field.

Founded in 1954 in San Francisco to prepare large print textbooks for partially seeing children, NAVH became the pioneer and standard setting agency in the preparation of large type.

Today, those publishers who meet our standards carry the prestigious "Seal of Approval" indicating high quality large print. We are delighted that Thorndike Press is one of the publishers whose titles meet these standards. We are also pleased to recognize the significant contribution Thorndike Press is making in this important and growing field.

Lorraine H. Marchi, L.H.D.
Founder/CEO
NAVH

* Thorndike Press encompasses the following imprints: Thorndike, Wheeler, Walker and Large Pr int Press.

ACKNOWLEDGMENTS

To Earl, my other half — for his husbandly love, encouragement, and help in a hundred ways.

To my research assistant, Shirley Bradley — for her expertise and enthusiasm.

To my editor, Natalee Rosenstein — for her faith in *The Cat Who* . . . from the very beginning.

To my literary agent, Blanche C. Gregory, Inc. — for a lifetime of agreeable partnership.

To the real-life Kokos and Yum Yums — for their fifty years of inspiration.

PROLOGUE

In Moose County, 400 miles north of everywhere, everyone likes Jim Qwilleran. Not only because he's a rich bachelor who likes to give his money away. Not only because he writes a lively column for the local newspaper. Not only because he dares to be different. (He lives alone, in a barn, with two cats.) True, he cuts a commanding figure: tall, well built, middle-aged, and adorned with a luxuriant moustache that is admired by men and adored by women. But the good folk of Moose County like Qwilleran because he listens!

As a journalist, he is trained to listen, and he never leaves home without a tape recorder in his pocket. Then, too, a sobering crisis in midlife has given him a sympathetic understanding reflected in his brooding gaze and his knack for saying the right thing.

According to his driver's license, he is James Mackintosh Qwilleran, spelled with a

Qw. To his friends he is "Qwill." To everyone else he is "Mr. Q."

Since relocating in Moose County, where the early settlers had been Scots, Qwilleran became aware of his Scottish heritage. (His mother had been a Mackintosh.) He wore a kilt on occasion, warmed to the sound of bagpipes, and quoted Robert Burns: "The best-laid schemes o' mice an' men / Gang aft agley." And he would explain, "It means the plans go haywire."

One particular summer his own plans were ambitious. Besides writing the twice-weekly "Qwill Pen" column for the *Moose County Something*, giving readings at public libraries of the new book he had just published, and starting to write another book . . . besides all these personal interests, he would help plan the Pickax City Sesquicentennial for the following year, take an interest in the new bookstore being built in Pickax — and more!

Then everything went haywire.

Chapter One

One of Qwilleran's "Qwill Pen" columns recently made this statement: "A town without a bookstore is like a chicken with one leg."

His devoted readers agreed — even those who had never bought a book in their life. And the Klingenschoen Foundation in Chicago, which managed Qwilleran's inheritance, considered a new bookstore a worthwhile investment.

For fifty years the late Eddington Smith had sold pre-owned books in a picturesque building behind the post office. Two days after his death it burned to the ground, and millions of printed pages were reduced to ashes. This would be the ideal site for a new bookstore. It was the end of an era and the beginning of a bright new adventure for readers. It would be built on the historic site where Eddington's grandfather had once shod horses and forged rims for wagon wheels. Perhaps that was not the black-smith's only means of supporting his family. There had long been rumors. . . .

All that aside, the site of the nineteenth-century smithy was to be the scene of a ceremonial groundbreaking. The good folk of Moose County liked special events: parades, barn raisings, livestock fairs, long funeral processions, and the like. They had never witnessed a formal groundbreaking. There would be a viewing stand for dignitaries, stirring music by the high school band, and a backhoe garlanded with flowers, to do the digging. It was suggested that the mayor should climb into the operator's seat and strike the first blow. Her Honor, Amanda Goodwinter, screamed, "Are you crazy? You couldn't get me on that blasted contraption with those silly flowers if you paid me!"

On Saturday vehicles streamed into Pickax from all directions. Newspapers in three counties were sending reporters and photographers. State police were called in to assist sheriff's deputies and Pickax police in handling the traffic. There had never been such a celebration in the history of Pickax!

Qwilleran was there, and he described it in his personal journal:

12

Saturday, May 31 — Eddington Smith would turn over in his grave! He was such a modest, honorable gentleman, and he would not want his grandmother's deathbed confession known. But there are no secrets in Moose County, and it seemed to be generally known that Eddington's grandfather was not only a blacksmith but a weekend pirate. He tied a red bandanna on his head and sailed under the black flag, preying on ships that brought gold coins to the New World for the purchase of the beaver pelts that were so much in demand in Europe. The rumor was that the loot was buried in a certain spot, now covered with asphalt.

So, instead of a few hundred spectators, there were a few thousand. County highways as well as city streets were clogged with sensation-seekers. Whole families attended — with picnic lunches and campstools. Would the pirate's loot be found? Or was it just a rumor? Bets were being placed among friends — nothing over a quarter. The idea was to have something "on the nose" to report to future generations.

Then sirens were heard! The state police were escorting TV teams who had unexpectedly flown up from Down Below in chartered planes. The media in metropolitan areas were always alert for bizarre happenings in the boondocks. And in the digital age, buried treasure was bizarre.

The high school band arrived in a school bus and proceeded to tune up noisily and discordantly for the next half hour, exciting the crowd.

The police strung their yellow tape around the digging area. The dignitaries entered the viewing stand. The backhoe operator was perched in the vehicle's lofty seat. Cops and deputies with sidearms entered the area and stood facing the crowd.

The band played "Stars and Stripes Forever," hitting most of the right notes, and the backhoe jockeyed into position. The boom rose, and the bucket dropped with a resounding crack. Onlookers seemed to be holding their collective breath as the machine backed and lunged, bashed and scraped and shoveled. Finally a shout rose from the crowd. The bucket brought up an iron-strapped chest.

Chief Andrew Brodie stepped forward and opened it. He spread his hands palms-down in a negative gesture. The chest was empty!

Groans of disappointment quickly turned into roars of laughter. The good folk of Moose County liked a good laugh, even at their own expense, and this was a good joke. The only ones who weren't laughing and crowing and whooping were the out-of-town media, and this tickled the locals even more; they liked to hoax outsiders.

Even old-timers in Pickax could not remember a year with so much excitement. The old opera house had been restored for the performing arts! Plans were under way for the city's Sesquicentennial celebration! The local soccer team had taken the championship away from Bixby County. And the K Fund was building a bookstore.

It was not just a rumor. The ground had already been broken. Polly Duncan, who had directed the public library for twenty years, was resigning in order to manage the new venture. She had gone to Chicago twice to consult the brain trust at the K Fund, as the philanthropic foundation was known.

There was also an incident of an unfortunate nature, but it was being hushed up. The body of a well-dressed man without identification had been found in a wooded area near the beach. He had been shot, execution-style. It happened on the day of the groundbreaking, and rumormongers were determined to find some connection but failed.

Qwilleran walked home from the groundbreaking. His barn was only a few blocks from downtown, but it was screened by a dense patch of woods. Though only a home address to a pair of pampered felines, it was an architectural wonder to residents of Moose County. An octagonal structure a century old, it rose from the barnyard like an ancient castle, four stories high and built of fieldstone and weathered wood siding.

Originally it had stored wagonloads of apples waiting to be pressed into cider. Now the lofts and ladders were gone, and so was the interior gloom. Odd-shaped windows had been cut into the siding at various levels, and all exposed wood surfaces — beams, rafters, and plank walls — had been bleached to a honey color.

There was living space on three balconies, connected by a ramp that spiraled up the interior wall. And in the center of the ground floor, a giant white fireplace cube served the living areas, with stacks rising to the roof forty feet overhead.

To the cats Qwilleran would say, "Be it ever so humble, there's no place like home."

In reply Koko would yowl and Yum Yum would sneeze delicately.

Now, as he arrived home from the groundbreaking, he looked for the welcoming committee sitting in the kitchen window. They were not there.

After unlocking the door, he found Yum Yum huddled on the blue cushion atop the refrigerator, looking worried. Koko paced the floor, looking uncomfortable.

"Something you ate?" Qwilleran asked in a jocular way.

Suddenly the cat uttered a bloodcurdling howl that started as a growl in his lower depths and ended in a shriek.

Qwilleran shuddered. He recognized Koko's "death howl"! Someone, somehow, somewhere was the victim of foul play.

There was no explanation, except that some cats, like some humans, seem to have psychic powers.

Koko and Yum Yum were a pair of purebred Siamese with pale fawn-colored bodies accented with seal-brown points. The male had a commanding appearance; the female was daintier and sweeter, although with a mind of her own. Both had the incredibly blue eyes of the breed.

Koko was the communicator of the family. He ordered meals, greeted guests, told them when to go home, and always, always spoke his mind, either in ear-piercing howls or an indecipherable *ik-ik-ik*.

They knew it was dinnertime and were throwing thought waves in Qwilleran's direction, sitting under the kitchen table and staring at their empty plates. He chopped turkey from the deli and watched them. Only once did Koko raise his head, and that was to stare at the wall telephone. A few seconds later, it rang. Polly Duncan, the chief woman in Qwilleran's life, was calling from Chicago, where she had been in conference with bigwigs at the Klingenschoen Foundation. She would be flying home the next morning. Qwilleran said he would pick her up at the airport and asked if she was bringing him something from the big city.

"Yes, and you'll love it!"

"What is it? Give me a clue."

"No clues. *À bientôt.*"

"*À bientôt.*"

Later that evening, when Qwilleran was reading a thought-provoking treatise from the *Wilson Quarterly*, Koko jumped onto a bookshelf and yowled; he wanted Qwilleran to read aloud. They enjoyed the sound of his voice, and Yum Yum liked to snuggle up to his rib cage and feel the vibrations. Koko went so far as to select the title, and Qwilleran read the one about the owl and the pussycat who went to sea in a beautiful pea-green boat, embellishing the lines with hoots, purrs, and meows. He thought, How can an animal who cannot read or understand the language . . . how can he choose one book over some other? It was something to ponder.

Polly's plane was due to arrive at noon on Sunday. In Moose County all shuttle flights from Chicago — or anywhere else — were consistently an hour late, and friends and relatives who met the passengers were consistently on time. They liked to stand around and make ludicrous comments about the service. They said:

"The tail fin was loose, and they'd run out of Scotch tape."

"The pilot had to have her hair done."

"They forgot to gas up and had to stop in Milwaukee. . . ."

The banter was an old Moose County custom, handed down from pioneer days, when a sense of humor helped the settlers cope with discomforts, hardships, and even disasters.

19

When the brave little plane finally bounced up to the terminal, Polly was the last one to disembark, descending the ramp warily, as if she believed the myth that it was built of recycled bicycle parts.

Qwilleran stepped forward, took her carry-on, and said he would collect her other luggage — if they could find the can opener to open the baggage compartment. They were discreet in their personal greetings; gossips were always watching for a sign of romance between the librarian and the newsman.

"Decent flight?"

"Bearable," she replied. "How was the groundbreaking?"

"Predictable. The chest was empty."

"It should go on permanent display in a glass case in the bookstore."

"Would you like to stop for brunch at Tipsy's?"

"I think not, dear," Polly said. "There has been much wining and dining, in addition to intensive work sessions. I just want to go home, hug my cats, have some cottage cheese and fruit, and get myself together for work tomorrow. . . . It's so peaceful here!"

They were driving to Indian Village, past sheep ranches, potato farms, and abandoned mine shafts. After a brief silence she added, "Benson is coming here this week."

"Who?"

"The architect of the bookstore. He wants to confer with the builders. And he's dying to see your barn. I described it, and he said it sounded architecturally impossible. He's a very interesting man."

Qwilleran huffed into his moustache. Every time Polly left Pickax, she met an "interesting" man. First it was the horse trainer in Lockmaster, then the professor in Montreal, and the antiques dealer in Virginia, and now an architect in Chicago.

Polly went on. "The K Fund thinks we should name the bookstore The Phoenix, after the mythical Egyptian bird that rose from the ashes and was reborn."

"Are they serious? The locals would want to know why we named it after the capital of Arizona. I think we should have a countywide contest for a name."

"I think you're right, but I wanted to hear you say it. . . . Did you look in on Brutus and Catta?"

"They're happy, but I believe your cat-sitter is overfeeding them. As you asked, I filled your refrigerator with everything on your list."

They were suddenly silent as they drove through the gates of Indian Village — past

21

the gatehouse on the right, past the club-house on the left, and onto River Road with its clusters of condos.

Qwilleran parked in front of Unit One of The Willows. "You run in and hug your cats," he said. "I'll take the luggage."

"Would you like to stay for some cottage cheese and fruit?" she asked in the soft, vibrant voice that had first attracted him. Cottage cheese was far from his favorite food. He hesitated a fraction of a second. "Yes, I believe I would."

Later in the afternoon Qwilleran took a legal pad and some yellow pencils — along with the Siamese and the cordless phone — to the gazebo. It was an octagonal summerhouse, screened on all eight sides — located in the bird garden a few yards from the barn. He drafted his Tuesday column; Yum Yum pursued her hobby of batting insects on the outside of the screen; Koko huddled on the floor and watched a family of seven crows strutting back and forth for his benefit. Were they the same ones that had visited the previous summer? Qwilleran wondered; all crows look alike, he thought. He called them the Bunkers, after Dr. Teresa Bunker, corvidologist. He considered her slightly nutty, like her cousin Joe, the

22

WPKX meteorologist. Joe called himself Wetherby Goode and spiced his weather predictions with jokes and jingles.

Qwilleran's ruminations were interrupted by a phone call.

It was his friend Thornton Haggis — retired stonecutter, history buff, and indefatigable volunteer.

"Hi, Qwill! Are you busy? I have something for you — and something to discuss."

"Where are you?"

"I've been helping out at the art center. I can be there in five minutes."

"We're in the gazebo. Care for a glass of wine?"

"Not tonight. We're having company. My wife invited the new pastor and a couple of people from the church."

The art center was at the far end of the former apple orchard, connected by an old wagon trail, and soon Thornton's shock of white hair, like a dust mop, could be seen approaching. The Siamese watched and waited with eagerness; they had never figured out the purpose of that white thing on his head.

Thornton was clutching what looked like a dumbbell, and he set it down on a table. "This is for you! A belated birthday present."

"It's spectacular!" Qwilleran said. "I can't believe you turned this on your lathe!"

Wood turning was Thornton's latest hobby.

"It's spalted olive wood. It's sort of a candy dish, but you can use it to feed the cats if you want to."

The Siamese were on the table, appraising the object with quivering noses. A saucer-like dish, over a sculpted stem and a round base, was turned from a single piece of wood, with the pronounced grain spiraling upward and ending in squizzles and splotches that nature had given to an olive tree.

Qwilleran said, "I'm overplussed and nonwhelmed, or vice versa. I'll keep it on my desk for stray paper clips, rubber bands, and gold coins. . . . Now, sit down and let's hear what's on your mind."

"Well, I know Pickax is a hundred and fifty years old next year, but the town of Brrr is two hundred years old *this year*. How to celebrate? The planning committee thinks that the average person is mixed up about 'centennial' and 'bicentennial' and 'sesqui-centennial.' So Brrr is going to have a simple birthday party in July and August. There'll be a birthday cake with two hundred candles, a parade of two hundred cabin

24

cruisers, and all kinds of shows and contests. The Reenactment Club will stage the Lumberjack Brawl in a saloon, and we're wondering if you'd take your one-man show out of mothballs and do it a couple of times during the summer. People are still talking about it!"

Thornton referred to the Big Burning of 1869, a forest fire that destroyed half of Moose County.

"Hmm," Qwilleran mused, stroking his moustache. "There was also a great storm of 1913 that sank scores of ships and destroyed lakefront towns."

"Perfect! Have you written it?"

"No, and that's the problem. For the show on the forest fire I had access to the Gage collection of historical documents. I've done no research on the 1913 storm."

"I'll do it for you," Thornton said with his usual enthusiasm. "Shall I tell Gary Pratt you're on the hook? Then you can take it from there."

Thornton got up to leave.

"What are you having for dinner tonight?"

"Something with leftover turkey. We're fond of turkey."

"Yow!" said Koko.

Thornton walked back to the Art Center.

As Qwilleran watched his friend walk down the lane, an idea struck him. He had recently collected twenty-seven Moose County legends to be published as a souvenir of the Sesquicentennial. Called *Short & Tall Tales*, the book was being printed privately by the Klingenschoen Foundation. Could it be ready in time for the Brrr birthday party?

He phoned the attorney G. Allen Barter at home. Bart, as he was called, represented Qwilleran in all matters pertaining to the K Fund.

"I can't foresee any problem," Bart said. "The text is in print; the slip-jacket has been designed."

"What color?" Qwilleran asked.

"They said it was something eye-catching."

Late that evening there was a phone call from Chief Brodie of the Pickax police force.

"Gotta talk to you!" he said in his gruff way. "Confidential!"

"Okay, Andy, come on over. Don't exceed the speed limit."

By the time the Scotch, ice cubes, and cheese tray were set up on the snack bar, the chief was there, stomping up to the bar with the same swaggering presence he had when in uniform. He sat at the bar and helped himself to the refreshments.

"You put on a good act at the ground-breaking, when you found the chest empty, Andy."

He grunted, like one unaccustomed to compliments.

Qwilleran asked, "Where is the empty chest now?"

"Locked up at the station, till they decide what to do with it. It should go on display at the new bookstore — in a bulletproof show-case. That's what they should call the book-store: The Pirate's Chest."

"Do you have any guess what happened to the contents?"

Brodie replied, "If there was anything in it when Eddington inherited, I say he con-verted it into government savings bonds and lived on them for the rest of his life. He sure didn't make enough money in the book business to keep his cat in sardines."

"But he was an astute bookman, Andy, despite his modest personality. Once in a while he probably bought a book for a dollar and sold it for a thousand. And he had a bookbinding business in the back room."

Qwilleran asked, "Well, anyway, what did you want to talk about?"

"The beach property you inherited from Fanny Klingenschoen. How far does it extend?"

"Half a mile — from Top o' the Dunes Club on the east to Cooper's Lane on the west. That's the dirt road with a boat launch at the end."

"Yeah. Used to be a hangout for kids until the sheriff cracked down."

"The entire K property is being placed in conservancy, but it hasn't been posted as yet. Why do you ask?"

The chief cut another wedge of cheese and poured another drink. "Mighty good cheese! . . . Well, a sheriff's deputy on patrol last night, just before dark, saw buzzards circling a patch of woods. She investigated and found a dead body on your property, about a hundred yards in from Cooper's Lane. Well-dressed male, shot in the back of the head, stripped of all ID. It'll be in the paper tomorrow, but I thought you'd like to know."

Qwilleran felt a familiar prickling sensation on his upper lip. "Any idea as to the time of death?"

"Interesting point. It was late afternoon, when everybody was at the groundbreaking, and all three police agencies were handling traffic."

"What are you implying, Andy? That it was a local job?"

"Or someone from Down Below trying to make it look like a local job. The SBI was called in. Don't say a word about this. What's the name of this cheese?"

"Port Salut, from the Sip and Nibble Shop."

Brodie grunted ambiguously. He gave Koko some morsels of cheese and was letting Yum Yum untie his shoes. The three of them had come a long way since their first awkward meeting.

Then, as the chief left, he said, "Let me know if your smart cat has any clues about this crime."

Brodie left, and Qwilleran realized that Koko's ghastly howl the previous afternoon really had been a death howl, and it signified wrongful death. It was happening thirty miles away! How did he know?

Qwilleran shook his head. One could go mad trying to figure out that cat! Was there a connection with something else? It was usually the case.

Chapter Two

The town of Brrr was not only the oldest in Moose County but also the coldest. (Visitors were warned not to go swimming or fall out of their boats.) It was also the most glamorous, in natural beauty and antiquity. There was a natural harbor, at the head of which soared a noble cliff, and on the cliff was a historic building with the unlikely name of Hotel Booze. Across its roof was a sign in letters that could be seen a mile into the lake: FOOD . . . ROOMS . . . BOOZE.

The Black Bear Café in the hotel served the best burgers in the county. At the entrance was a mounted bear rising menacingly on hind legs, and the proprietor had an ursine appearance himself, with his shuffling gait and shaggy black hair and beard.

On Monday morning Qwilleran phoned the innkeeper, Gary Pratt, to talk about Brrr's birthday party, and was not surprised to be invited to lunch. The café had a down-to-earth shabbiness that appealed to boaters, fishermen, and campers, and the high stools at the long bar were appropriately rickety.

Gary was behind the bar. "Want to have your burger at the bar, Qwill? Then we can talk."

"It's smart of you to call it a birthday party instead of a bicentennial," Qwilleran said. "It's in keeping with the personality of the town and will appeal to your kind of tourists."

"It's crazy, but we can get away with it because we're fifty years older than Pickax. Their shindig'll be pretty grand, I hear. We can do things they can't — like a parade of two hundred cabin cruisers, each flying an American flag. It's gonna be a fantastic spectacle. The TV crews will be up here from Down Below."

"Do you have that many cabin cruisers?"

"Sure do! They're signing up already — from towns all along the beach. And for the kids, we're building a ten-foot wooden birthday cake with two hundred electric candles — make a wish and blow, and the candles go out! Thing of it is, we can do stunts like this that would be too crazy for Pickax."

For a while Gary left to tend bar, and Qwilleran enjoyed the burger called "bear burger" by the regulars. Then they discussed the show on the Great Storm. It would be staged in the hotel ballroom, same as the show on the Big Burning.

"You may remember, Gary, that I had an assistant to handle the tape recorder and bring in music or voices on cue. Can we get Nancy Fincher to do it again? She was very good."

"Too bad," Gary said. "Nancy married a dogsledder who races in the Iditarod, and she moved to Minnesota with her thirty Siberian huskies. But I know a guy who could do a good job for you."

"A woman is better, Gary — for visual balance and interest. She'd have to be available for rehearsals — to get the timing down pat. Timing is everything."

"Excuse me a minute." Gary moved down the bar and served an early luncher and two early drinkers.

Qwilleran was drinking Squunk water, a mineral water from a local spring.

When Gary shuffled back with a plate of apple pie, he said, "Did you ever happen to meet Lish Carroll? I think she left town before you came up here."

Qwilleran said, "I can safely say I've never

in my life met anyone called Lish."

"Short for Alicia," the barkeeper said. "She's my age. I knew her in high school. A sharp cookie — into science, math, computers — all A's. I steered clear of that type."

Gary said, "Funny thing, I remember that she had very small feet, and when the guys teased her about it, she said that people with small feet have large brains, and she looked pointedly at the gunboats they were wearing. Lish was never subtle!"

"She left town after high school, but she's back now, visiting her grandmother. Don't know how long she'll be here, but she'd be the right one to press buttons on cue for your show."

"Where does she live?"

"Milwaukee, I think."

"Milwaukee?" Qwilleran had a suppressed desire to talk with a Milwaukeean and ask some questions — just to satisfy his curiosity. Nothing serious.

"What is this smart cookie's profession, may I ask?"

"I don't know exactly. There's always been a lot of gossip about her. Excuse me." Gary signaled to a waitress who was setting up tables and pointed to the customers at the bar. Then he said to Qwilleran, "Let's go into my office."

Qwilleran's interest was piqued. Lish sounded promising.

Gary shut the door and poured two mugs of coffee from his personal carafe. It proved to be somewhat better than the brew served in the restaurant. In Qwilleran's book "stronger" meant "better."

"The thing of it is," Gary began, "Lish lived with her grandma in Brrr while she was in high school. She even took her grandmother's last name. Perhaps you know old Mrs. Carroll who lives in the house that looks like Mount Vernon. No? There was a scandal, you see, in Lockmaster, where Lish had grown up. Her father was a big-shot landowner, and her mother was a social snob. Then he went to prison for land fraud — on a grand scale! — and a female employee was involved, one way or another. His wife was so stunned or embarrassed or something that she overdosed. And Lish landed in Brrr with her grandmother."

"Do you expect me to believe this, Gary? It sounds like something you read in a tabloid."

"Honest! It was all over the *Lockmaster Ledger* when it happened. More coffee? So now the scuttlebutt is that old Mrs. Carroll is moving into Ittibittiwassee Estates, and

Lish is getting the big house. Do you want to hear more?"

"I never say no to coffee or scuttlebutt, Gary."

"Well, the thing of it is, Lish travels with a guy, and that doesn't set too well with Grandma Carroll. Lish says he's her driver; she can't have a license because of a special heart condition. He's tall and lanky, and you see him traipsing behind her like a puppy dog."

"Do they come in here? Is Lish good-looking?"

"Well, she has . . . an intelligent face. Her driver is good-looking and has long hair and drinks a lot. I call them Lish and Lush."

Qwilleran went home and thought about the brainy young woman with an intelligent face. No doubt she could handle the sound effects skillfully, but he had hoped for someone with an engaging personality. There was, however, one detail in her favor. She lived, or had lived, in Milwaukee.

Qwilleran's interest in the brainy young woman was understandable, but he needed a second opinion. He called his friend Wetherby Goode, a native of Lockmaster.

"Qwill! Where've you been? I haven't

seen you since you moved back to the barn!"

The two men had adjoining condos in Indian Village, and Qwilleran spent winters there when the barn was too hard to heat.

"I need to talk to you, Joe. How about coming over for sandwiches and coffee — between your six p.m. and eleven p.m. broadcasts. Lois's Luncheonette is featuring TLTs this week, and it's turkey off the bone."

The Siamese hopped about joyously when the weatherman's car pulled into the barnyard. Did they recognize the sound of the motor from last winter in Indian Village? Did they sense that the driver lived with a cat named Jet Stream? Did they know what was in the sandwiches that had been delivered?

The reunion consisted of loud talk and backslapping. Then they trooped out to the gazebo, with the host carrying a large tray and the guest carrying the cats and a cordless phone in a canvas tote bag.

"Did you attend the groundbreaking?" Qwilleran asked.

"No, I had a family powwow to attend in Horseradish, but I read all about it in today's paper."

Qwilleran surmised that the personable bachelor had found a new attraction in his hometown in addition to his ample supply of cousins, aunts, nieces, uncles, nephews, and in-laws.

Wetherby went on, "I'll bet Polly is all excited about managing the store. What will they name it? How about The Pirate's Chest? I hope they're planning to have a cat. If they want music at the grand opening, I'd be glad to play."

"Do you have a repertory of bookstore music, Joe?"

"Without giving it any deep thought, I'd say that . . . John Field's *Nocturnes* would be good for starters."

"Yow!" said Koko, who had been sitting nearby.

"See? He agrees with me," Wetherby said.

"Don't be fooled, Joe. Koko saw a sliver of turkey drop out of your sandwich."

"Hey, Qwill! I never told you how much I enjoyed your column on *Cool Koko!*"

He referred to a recent "Qwill Pen" column in which Qwilleran introduced the wise sayings of *Cool Koko:* "A cat with no tail is better than a politician with no head. . . . A cat may look at a king, but he doesn't have to lick his boots. . . . Every dog has his day, but cats have three hundred sixty-five."

He said to Wetherby, "If Jet Stream has

37

any wise sayings, send them to *Cool Koko,* in care of the *Moose County Something.*" Then he mentioned casually, "Do you happen to remember, Joe, a big land-fraud scandal in Lockmaster?"

"Sure do! The Kranson case. Juiciest crime we ever had in our simon-pure county! Why do you ask?"

"To answer your question in a roundabout way: Do you remember the one-man show I did on the Big Burning?"

"I should! I saw it three times!"

"Well, I'm doing a similar dramatization on the Great Storm of 1913, and the Kranson daughter has been suggested to handle the sound effects."

"Sorry. Don't know anything about her."

"Oh," Qwilleran said, "I thought you might, since you spend so much of your time in Horseradish."

The sly comment was overlooked — or purposely avoided — as the weatherman jumped up, tapped his watch, said he was due at the station, said a hasty thanks for the food, and left.

It was Tuesday before Polly felt "settled" enough to enjoy a dinner date. She left the library early, had her hair done, splurged on a facial, and went home to

38

put on the summer suit she had bought in Chicago. The color was called "orange sherbet," and she felt quite daring.

When Qwilleran arrived to pick her up, he exclaimed, "You look . . . wonderful!" It was the only adjective he knew that meant radiant, well coiffed, and well dressed.

"And you look handsome," she murmured. He had trimmed his moustache and coordinated his blazer, shirt, and tie. Dressing carefully was a compliment they paid each other — and the restaurant — when they dined out.

They went to the Old Grist Mill, which combined country charm with contemporary chic. The owner, Elizabeth Hart, was from Chicago. Her maître d', Derek Cuttlebrink, was from the town of Wildcat.

"You guys look spiffy tonight," he said with the nervy nonchalance of a favorite son who is six-feet-eight. "What'll it be? One dry sherry and one Q cocktail straight up?" He handed them the cards with a conspiratorial whisper. "Avoid the lamb curry unless you want to live dangerously."

When the drinks were served, Qwilleran said, "Now tell me how things are going at the library."

"We hired a very nice woman to be my successor, Myrtle Parsons. She was a school librarian in Bixby, and is so happy to be working here. We're working together on everything that comes up. Last night she attended the monthly dinner meeting with the Dear Ladies, and they were very charming to her."

"Dear Ladies" was Polly's nickname for the white-haired, conventional, wealthy, and charming members of the board of directors.

Qwilleran said, "You may be able to leave the library sooner than you anticipated."

"Oh, I hope so. The people at the K Fund have given me a six-hundred-page book to study. Everything from accounting procedures to zone and cluster plans."

The appetizers were served. Qwilleran had french-fried oysters. Polly had tomato consommé. Too lemony, she said.

"The design of the building is exciting — a long, narrow building with an entrance that's quite inviting. All windows will be clerestory or skylights; all wall space is devoted to bookshelves. Although there'll be an elevator to the lower level, there'll also be a rather grand staircase — the kind people like to walk down."

"What will be downstairs?"

Her answer was interrupted by the arrival of the entrées. Qwilleran had bravely ordered the lamb curry. Polly had poached salmon with yogurt sauce, a twice-baked potato, and asparagus. She said the portions were too large.

Part of the lower level, Qwilleran knew, would be the Eddington Smith Room, offering pre-owned books donated by local families. It would be staffed by volunteers, and proceeds would go to the Literacy Fund. Then there would be an all-purpose room for book signings and a literary club like the one in Lockmaster. The Lit Club sponsored by the *Lockmaster Ledger* featured visiting speakers, book reviews, and some lively discussion. Qwilleran was often invited to speak.

Polly said, "There will also be a display case for exhibiting treasures behind glass: rare books and manuscripts, and collections of things related to reading and writing. These will be loaned by antique shops and private individuals."

"No food?" Qwilleran asked.

"No food, no gifts. Just around the corner are a gift shop and an ice cream parlor."

For dessert they ordered blackberry cobbler. Polly said it looked awfully rich.

"But I have been doing all the talking, Qwill. What has kept you occupied?" she asked absently.

"Not much," he said. "What did you bring me from the big city?"

"A CD recording of Massenet's piano pieces. They'll sound wonderful on your big sound system."

"Good!" he said. "Shall we go to the barn and listen to music?"

Qwilleran could have told Polly about his plans for the next day, but Polly was so thrilled about the bookstore and everything concerning it that he had no desire to dampen her enthusiasm. He had never seen her so animated!

The next evening he would drive to Lockmaster for the first book signing in how many years? Earlier in his life, while a crime reporter Down Below, he had authored a book titled *City of Brotherly Crime*. Since then, none of his ideas had jelled until he moved to Moose County and discovered the wealth of legends originating from pioneer days, to be published as *Short & Tall Tales*.

In Lockmaster, the adjoining county, he had many friends and readers of the "Qwill Pen" column, and Kip MacDiarmid, editor of the *Lockmaster Ledger*, had arranged for a book signing on the eve of publication. It would be a private preview for members of the local Literary Club and would be held in the community room of the local bookstore.

The room was crowded with members of the club; the editor's introduction was flattering, and applause was vociferous, and someone shouted, "Where's Koko?"

Qwilleran walked to the lectern, surveyed the audience at length with his brooding eyes, then stroked his oversized moustache. His silence brought a standing ovation.

Then he began to speak in his mellifluous voice: "This is the story of a woman who put fear into the male population of a small town in Moose County. It is a true tale, as told by Gary Pratt, proprietor of the Hotel Booze in the Scottish town of Brrr."

The audience began to wriggle in delight and anticipation. Qwilleran proceeded to bring alive the legend, imitating the high-pitched voice of the hotel proprietor.

HILDA THE CLIPPER

My grandfather used to tell about this eccentric old woman in Brrr who had everybody terrorized. This was about seventy years ago, you understand. She always walked around town with a pair of hedge clippers, pointing them at people and going *click-click* with the blades. Behind her back they laughed and called her Hilda the

Clipper, but the same people were very nervous when she was around.

The thing of it was, nobody knew if she was just an oddball or was really smart enough to beat the system. In stores she picked up anything she wanted without paying a cent. She broke all the town ordinances and got away with it. Once in a while a cop or the sheriff would question her from a safe distance, and she said she was taking her hedge clippers to be sharpened. She didn't have a hedge. She lived in a tar-paper shack with a mangy dog. No electricity, no running water. My grandfather had a farmhouse across the road, and Hilda's shack was on his property. She lived there rent-free, brought water in a pail from his hand pump, and helped herself to firewood from his woodpile in winter.

One night, right after Halloween, the Reverend Mr. Wimsey from the church here was driving home from a prayer meeting at Squunk Corners. It was a cold night, and cars didn't have heaters then. His Model T didn't even have side curtains, so he was dressed warm. He was chugging along the country road, at probably twenty miles an hour, when he saw somebody in the darkness ahead, trudging down the middle of the dirt road and wearing a bathrobe and bedroom slippers. She was carrying hedge clippers.

Mr. Wimsey knew her well. She'd been a member of his flock until he suggested she quit bringing the clippers to services. Then she gave up going to church and was kind of hostile. Still, he couldn't leave her out there to catch her death of cold. Nowadays you'd just call the sheriff, but there were no car radios then, and no cell phones. So he pulled up and asked where she was going.

"To see my friend," she said in a gravelly voice.

"Would you like a ride, Hilda?"

She gave him a mean look and then said, "Seein' as how it's a cold night . . ." She climbed in the car and sat with the clippers on her lap and both hands on the handles.

Mr. Wimsey told Grandpa he gulped a couple of times and asked where her friend lived.

"Over yonder." She pointed across a cornfield.

"It's late to go visiting," he said. "Wouldn't you rather I should take you home?"

"I told you where I be wantin' to go," she shouted, as if he was deaf, and she gave the clippers a *click-click*.

"That's all right, Hilda. Do you know how to get there?"

"It's over yonder." She pointed to the left.

At the next road he turned left and drove for about a mile without seeing anything like a house. He asked what the house looked like.

"I'll know it when we get there!" *Click-click*.

"What road is it on? Do you know?"

"It don't have a name." *Click-click*.

"What's the name of your friend?"

"None o' yer business! Just take me there."

She was shivering, and he stopped the car and started taking off his coat. "Let me put my coat around you, Hilda."

"Don't you get fresh with me!" she shouted, pushing him away and going *click-click*.

Mr. Wimsey kept on driving and thinking what to do. He drove past a sheep pasture, a quarry, and dark farmhouses with barking dogs. The lights of Brrr glowed in the distance, but if he steered in that direction, she went into a snit and clicked the clippers angrily.

Finally he had an inspiration. "We're running out of fuel!" he said in an anxious voice. "We'll be stranded out here! We'll freeze to death! I have to go into town to buy some gasoline!"

It was the first time in his life, he told Grandpa, that he'd ever told a lie, and he prayed silently for forgiveness. He also prayed the trick would work. Hilda didn't object. Luckily she was getting drowsy, probably in the first stages of hypothermia. Mr. Wimsey found a country store and went in to use their crank telephone.

In two minutes a sheriff deputy drove up on a motorcycle. "Mr. Wimsey! You old rascal!" he said to the preacher. "We've been looking all over for the Clipper! Better talk fast, or I'll have to arrest you for kidnapping!"

What happened, you see: Hilda's dog had been howling for hours, and Grandpa called the sheriff.

Eventually Hilda was lodged in a foster home — for her own protection — and had to surrender her hedge clippers. The whole town breathed a lot easier. I asked my grandfather why they put up with her eccentricities for so long. He said, "Folks still had the pioneer philosophy: Shut up and make do!"

Qwilleran was gratified by the cordial welcome of the Literary Club, their response to his reading, and the number of books presented for signing. He regretted only that it could not happen in Pickax at The Pirate's Chest — as it was destined to be named.

Chapter Three

It was Thursday — time to write another thousand words for the "Qwill Pen" column — and Qwilleran's head was devoid of ideas. That meant resorting to the Koko System. The man yelled "Book!" and the cat came running — leaping onto a bookshelf, sniffing bindings, and nudging a selected title off the shelf. And that became the topic for the "Qwill Pen."

Qwilleran would be the first to admit that the system was ludicrous . . . but it was simple, and it worked. It gave Koko pleasure, and it gave Qwilleran a challenge. He boasted that he could write a thousand words about anything — or nothing.

On this occasion, the chosen book was *The Tiger in the House* by Carl Van Vechten, one of the last pre-owned classics that Qwilleran had purchased from the late Eddington Smith. Its cover looked rain-soaked, the spine was tattered, and the gold tooling had worn off, but its three hundred pages were intact, printed on India laid paper, in a limited edition of two thousand, dated 1920.

This copy was signed by the author.

Qwilleran described it in his column as a superb literary work, a scholarly history of the domestic cat, beginning almost forty centuries ago in Egypt. There were names of famous artists and statesmen who cherished the cat as a household pet. And there were the names of tyrants and murderers who hated or feared the very mention of the animal. Particularly interesting were the myths and superstitions that persisted throughout the centuries.

Qwilleran himself, living with a cat that seemed to be psychic, was encouraged in his belief by attitudes in the Orient, where cats were considered supernatural. In Siam they were considered to be royalty. He had long wanted to trace Koko's ancestry. Readers of the "Qwill Pen" knew Koko to be a smart cat, but even close friends like Polly and Arch had not been told the whole story — for the simple reason that they would scoff. A detective lieutenant Down Below did not scoff; the Pickax police chief had been gradually convinced; and a retired police detective from California was ready to be converted. Qwilleran found it a curious fact that they were all members of the constabulary!

The prospect of doing another one-man show for a Moose County audience filled Qwilleran with elation. He remembered audience reaction to the first one: They were spellbound; they gasped; they cried. In college he had focused on theater training before switching to journalism, and he still relished the idea of using his voice dramatically to influence an audience.

Now, to refresh his memory, he reviewed the script of the Big Burning. The audience had been told to imagine that radio actually existed in 1869, as he announced the news of the disaster, read bulletins from other parts of the county, and interviewed eyewitnesses by telephone.

Radio was still in the future at the time of the Great Storm — 1913. There were no broadcasting stations, no home receivers using cat whiskers, no commercials for tin lizzies or potbellied stoves. Then he thought, Why not add to the realism with a few commercials? There could be bargains in kerosene and ten-pound bags of oatmeal.

In 1913 Moose County had no real newspaper — only the *Pickax Picayune*, with social notes and classified ads. Lockmaster County, to the south, was further advanced. Qwilleran phoned his friend Kip MacDiarmid, editor of the *Lockmaster Ledger*.

"Kip! Do me a big favor. Meet me for lunch at Inglehart's and bring some photocopies of the *Ledger* of 1913. The lunch is on me!"

"Good deal!" said the editor. "Which pages and how many?"

"Just three or four. Inside pages with display ads for groceries, clothing, hardware — whatever."

The two newsmen met at the restaurant in a Victorian mansion on Lockmaster's main thoroughfare and were given a table by a window hung with lace curtains. Kip had a glass of wine; Qwilleran asked for Squunk water on the rocks with a twist but settled for club soda. He knew no one south of the border had ever heard of Squunk water.

"Your groundbreaking was a great show," Kip said. "Did you know the chest was empty?"

"No one had the foggiest idea!"

"I hope you're going to call the bookstore

The Pirate's Chest. Is Polly excited about running it?"

"Rather!" Qwilleran said. "She looks twenty years younger. And by the way, she wants to know how you run your literary club. She wants to start one at the bookstore."

"I'll have Moira get in touch with her; she's secretary of the Lit Club."

Qwilleran asked, "Have you heard about the Bicentennial of the town of Brrr? I'm doing a show on the Great Storm of 1913. That's why I asked for some 1913 clips of the *Ledger*."

"Did you know it was called the *Lockmaster Logger* then?"

They chatted, stopping long enough to order lunch. Kip recommended the turkey potpie, made with bacon and turnips.

Qwilleran said he'd stick to his favorite Reuben sandwich.

"Are you going to write another book, Qwill?"

"Well, off the record, I'm writing *The Private Life of the Cat Who* . . . Just a series of sketches of my experiences with two Siamese. Don't tell Polly. She'd think it too frivolous. She wants me to write a literary masterpiece that will win the Pulitzer Prize. How is Moira? We should all have dinner at the Mackintosh Inn sometime."

"Good idea! Did you know that Moira is breeding marmalade cats? She wants to know if you're going to have a bookstore cat. If so, she'd like to present you with a pedigreed marmalade."

Qwilleran hesitated. He had known some scruffy, overweight orange cats in his time, and he said warily, "That's a decision for Polly to make. It's a good thought, though; books and cats go together."

"I'll tell Moira to phone Polly. I know it's a little premature, since you've only just dug the hole for the building. But Moira has a handsome devil in the cattery, a few months old, and she would save him for you if Polly's interested. She said he's a people cat, born to win friends and influence customers. When do you expect the store to open?"

"Before snow flies."

"Meanwhile, have you opened your log cabin yet?"

"I've alerted the janitorial service to get it ready for summer."

"I hear there was a murder in the woods near your place. Are you ready with an alibi?"

They rambled on, and the banter reminded Qwilleran of lunches at the Press

Club Down Below, when he was an under-paid hack working for the *Daily Fluxion.* "Let's do this again, Kip," he said when they parted.

"And let's not wait so long next time!"

Only when Qwilleran was driving back to Pickax did he realize he had forgotten to ask about the land-fraud scandal in Lockmaster — and an orphaned daughter who had changed her name and moved to Moose County.

At the barn the Siamese were waiting expectantly, as if they knew he was bringing some tasty fragments of Reuben sandwich. Then he locked himself in his writing studio on the first balcony with a thermal coffee decanter, there to write a "Qwill Pen" column for the following week. It would be about June.

He made notes:

- June is bustin' out all over. (Show)
- What is so rare as a day in June? (Poem)
- A four-letter word, but a polite one.
- The month of weddings, graduations, and the second income-tax estimate.

His note-taking was interrupted by a

phone call from Polly, in high spirits.

"Qwill, dear! You'll never guess what happened today."

"How many guesses —" he began but was interrupted. He had never known Polly to be so voluble.

"Moira MacDiarmid phoned to offer the bookstore a marmalade cat for a mascot! One with a real Scottish heritage! A genuine people cat! Just what we'll need to welcome customers and make them feel at home!"

"Male or female?" he questioned with the fact-finding instincts of a newsman.

"A little boy. Breeders call their kittens little boys and little girls, you know. He's several months old and will be a yearling when the store is ready to open."

"What does he look like?"

"His coat is soft and dense and huggable, Moira says. His color is a rich cream with tabby markings in soft apricot! And he has large green eyes! Can't you imagine him, Qwill, against a background of lively green carpet — lively green, not the somber forest green used in public places, although Fran Brodie may not approve. She has her own ideas, you know."

"The K Fund is hiring her to design the interior," he said. "Just tell them what you want, and they'll tell her! And that's the way

56

it will be!" He detected a sigh of satisfaction. There had never been a friendly rapport between the designer and Polly — or between the designer and Yum Yum, for that matter.

"Then you approve, Qwill?"

"Provided he doesn't turn out to be one of those thirty-pound marmalades that get all the publicity."

"No! No!" Polly assured him. "Dundee has good genes."

"Dundee? Is that his name?"

"Isn't that adorable?" Polly said. "Especially since his ancestors came from the city associated with orange marmalade! Well, I had to call you. The news was too good to keep."

"I'm glad you did, Polly."

"*À bientôt,*" she said in the voice that was always full of warmth and meaning.

"*À bientôt.*" He leaned back in his chair and let his mind wander.

A few moments passed, and then he was aware of a slight commotion beyond his door. Whenever the Siamese wanted to attract his attention, they staged a cat squabble. He opened his door and they tumbled into the room.

"You fakers!" he scolded.

They scampered down the ramp to the broom closet on the main floor. Their message was clear. They had been shut up indoors for too long.

A canvas tote bag advertising the Pickax Public Library was brought from the closet, and they jumped inside, contracting their bodies and snuggling together to fit in the bottom of the bag. They had no objection to being buried under some magazines, a bottle of Squunk water, a cordless phone, some writing materials, and a worn-out necktie. It was all part of a trip to the gazebo, a journey that lasted the better part of a minute. Then they hopped out of the conveyance and prepared for a game of Nip the Necktie.

Qwilleran moved some furniture to provide a suitable arena, then swished the tie through the air — back and forth, up and down, around in circles — while the cats leaped, grabbed, missed, fell on their backs, shook themselves off, and leaped again.

When they had had enough, they crept away to their favorite corners of the gazebo to watch anything that moved on the other side of the screen panels.

Qwilleran did some more hard thinking about the month of June. He could invite his readers to compose original jingles about the sixth month. As prizes he would offer the usual yellow lead pencils with "Qwill

Pen" stamped in gold.

As he brainstormed, he became aware of a familiar chattering sound: *"ik-ik-ik."* Koko reserved it for snakes, large dogs, and trespassers with hunting rifles. Both cats were staring at the shrubbery in the bird garden. Qwilleran stared, too. He had only his eyes; the cats had their sixth sense.

As he concentrated there was movement in the dense foliage, and three long-legged birds emerged. They were the strangest he had ever seen — long snakelike necks, small ugly heads, scrawny bodies, and those long, scaly legs!

They surveyed the scene calmly, as if they considered buying the property . . . until an unearthly roar and shriek from Koko's throat sent them back into the shrubbery.

The three in the gazebo were speechless: the cats with bushed tails, and Qwilleran with exactly the same sensation in his moustache. His first thought, upon returning to rationality, was to call Thornton Haggis, who had lived in Moose County all his life and knew all the answers — or where to get them. Recently named Volunteer of the Year, Thorn could always be found pushing wheelchairs at the Senior Care Facility or manning the reception desk at the hospital. Qwilleran found him answering phones at the Art Center.

"Just holding the fort while the manager gets her hair done," he said. "I bet I know why you're calling, Qwill. About the research on the Great Storm! I've done all the legwork, and now I'm organizing the material for you. I can drop it off at the barn tomorrow. Will you be there?"

"If I'm not, you can leave it in the old sea chest." Outside the kitchen door there was a weathered wood chest for receiving package deliveries, catered food, and — once — two abandoned kittens.

"By the way, Thorn, I had a strange experience a few minutes ago. I was in the gazebo when three ugly-looking birds walked out of the woods." He described them. "And they were between two and three feet tall. And weird-looking. They had red pouches hanging from heads that can only be described as rapacious."

After a moment's silence, Thorn said facetiously, "What did you have to drink for lunch, Qwill? They sound like wild turkeys, but we don't have wild turkeys in Moose County — not for the last thirty years. My sons are experienced game-bird hunters, and they have to go to Minnesota or Upper Michigan for wild turkeys."

"Interesting," Qwilleran said. "The cats

saw them, too. Koko snarled like a dragon and frightened them away."

Qwilleran had long wanted to find an explanation for Koko's remarkable intuition. Now he expressed his thoughts in a letter to himself, in his personal journal.

Thursday, June 12 — I've been reading *The Tiger in the House* again. Beautiful work! I've always wanted to write a scholarly tome requiring years of research, but I lack the temperament.

The book inspired me, however, to pursue the mystery of Koko's heritage. Is he descended from the supernormal lines of old Siam? How many generations have passed between him and his royal ancestors? What do I know about him? Very little. Only that he lived Down Below with a man named Mountclemens, who apparently acquired him from a sister in Milwaukee.

I was writing for the *Daily Fluxion* and renting an apartment from the art critic, who owned an old Victorian mansion. He called himself George Bonifield Mountclemens the Third. He was a pompous donkey!, and no one really believed his name. But he lived upstairs among his art treasures with a Siamese cat named Kao K'o Kung. When Mountclemens was killed, the cat moved in with me and became known as Koko.

But I always thought, If I ever meet anyone from Milwaukee, I'll ask some questions: Is there a Mountclemens family there? Is there a cat breeder specializing in Siamese in Milwaukee?

This "Lish" person may be the one to ask.

Chapter Four

On Friday morning Qwilleran finished writing his discourse on the month of June, making it a little shorter than the traditional thousand words. In the last few weeks he had appended his column with a few words of catly wisdom from *Cool Koko's Almanac*.

"Cool Koko says: Half a dish of cream is better than none. . . . Opportunity only knocks once; grab that pork chop while no one's looking. . . . Why sing for your supper? It's easier just to stare at your empty plate."

The "Cool Koko" stunt had started when Qwilleran was researching Benjamin Franklin for his column and decided to parody *Poor Richard's Almanack*. It had been intended as a one-time spoof, but readers loved Cool Koko and clamored for more. He had obliged with: "Man works from sun to sun, but cats get by without lifting a paw. . . . A dog by any other name would smell like a dog. . . . Dumb animals know more about humans than dumb humans know about animals."

Qwilleran, who admitted to having a short attention span, was tired of writing about Cool Koko. The mailroom at the news office was swamped with postcards suggesting bits of catly wisdom. The editor, Arch Riker, accused Qwilleran of trying to start a new cult.

And so, on that Friday, the "Qwill Pen" ended with an announcement in boldface caps:

COOL KOKO
IS ON VACATION INDEFINITELY

Then, with a light heart, Qwilleran went to the beach, taking the Siamese.

It was only a brief inspection trip; O'Dell's cleaning crew had been there to air it out, wash windows, check the facilities, dust, and sweep. It was to be hoped they had also tidied the driveway and grounds of fallen branches.

The Siamese went along, contentedly snuggled in their carrying coop. How did they know they were going to the beach and not to the vet? They could smell the lake a mile before they reached the shore and made small pleasurable noises.

When they reached the lakeshore, the highway dipped in and out, with occasional glimpses of the vast expanse of blue water. The noise in the backseat increased. Then the car turned off into the K property on a dirt driveway that wound through a dense growth of wild cherries and scrub oaks, emerging on the crest of a sand dune.

There stood the venerable log cabin with its mammoth fieldstone chimney and magnificent view of the lake. The occupants of the carrier thumped around, rattled the door, and squealed with joy.

Qwilleran went indoors first to be sure everything was secure, then brought in the cats. It would take them an hour to sniff the two screened porches, the rugs and furniture of the interior, the hand-hewn mantel over the stone fireplace, the rafters overhead, the accoutrements of their feeding station, the gravel in their commode, and their empty water dish, which was quickly filled.

The refrigerator was empty, except for ice cubes, but Qwilleran had brought treats in a cooler.

On the lake porch there was a railroad tie upended and nailed to a base — intended as a pedestal for a copper sculpture of a sailboat. But Koko had claimed it as his own viewing post from which he could monitor the waving beach grasses, the beach at the foot of the dune, seagulls fighting over a dead fish, and beachcombers looking for agates. It was early season for traffic on the beach, but one couple wandered past: a young woman walking with a hiker's stride and swinging arms, while a tall, lanky man shuffled along behind her, his hands in his hip pockets.

Qwilleran, who knew all the cottagers in the Top o' the Dunes Club to the east, sized the strangers up as newcomers, guests of the regulars. When they returned a few minutes later and stopped to stare up at the cabin, he kept very quiet and motionless. The woman pointed to the cabin, as strangers often did, marveling at the age of the building or the size of the stone chimney. Strangers often pointed to the cats; some people, unfortunately, thought of Siamese as being an expensive breed, worth stealing, and Koko and Yum Yum were never allowed on the screened porch without a chaperone.

At any rate, the woman pointed and spoke to her companion at length, and he nodded without showing much interest.

It never occurred to Qwilleran that they

were Lish and "Lush."

Koko had reacted to them with a half-growl, but that was not unusual. Whenever a finger was pointed at him, he resented it. Compliments were graciously accepted, but there was something about a pointing finger that insulted his feline sensibilities. . . . Cats! Who could understand them!

Sunday noon Qwilleran and Polly drove to the Top o' the Dunes Club to have brunch with the Rikers, their best friends. Arch was the somewhat paunchy editor-in-chief of the newspaper; Mildred was the plumply pretty editor of the food page. It was a late marriage for them, both having survived domestic disasters.

The club was simply a row of cottages overlooking a hundred miles of blue water and bearing names like "Sunny Daze" and "Many Pines" and "No Oaks." The Riker cottage was bright yellow with black shutters and a broad deck cantilevered over the slope of the dune. On the wide top rail of the deck sat Toulouse, a fluffy black-and-white stray who had wandered into Mildred's life. Qwilleran, upon arrival, always stroked Toulouse and told him he was a handsome brute.

Polly said, "He's always the epitome of contentment!"

"He should be!" Qwilleran said. "He was a dirty, half-starved stray when he moved in with the food writer of the *Moose County Something*. As Cool Koko would say, if he were not on vacation, *'There's a destiny that leads hungry cats to the right doorstep.'*"

Then the Comptons arrived via the beach and climbed the sand-ladder up the slope of the dune. Lyle had been school superintendent for twenty years, and his forays with teachers, parents, and the school board had given him a professional scowl, although it masked a good sense of humor.

His nickname in the school system was Scrooge. The name of their cottage was "Bah! Humbug!"

Lisa had retired from school administration with the sunny optimism of a Campbell whose ancestors had founded Brrr two hundred years before.

It was a balmy June day — the sunshine gentle, the breezes soft, the temperature just right, so aperitifs were served on the open deck overlooking the lake.

Lisa said, "Oh, Qwill! Aren't we going to have any more of Cool Koko's wisdom? It was so much fun."

He said, "I'm hoping that readers will be

inspired to invent their own Kokoisms. I've got to go on to other things."

"Such as what?" Lyle asked.

"Such as a script for a one-man show on the Great Storm of 1913 — for the Brrr anniversary. Thornton Haggis has done the research. The format will be similar to 'The Big Burning.' And Gary Pratt has recommended Mrs. Carroll's granddaughter, Alicia Carroll, to handle the sound effects." He waited for a reaction.

"Is she back in town?" Mildred asked in surprise. "I talked to Mrs. Carroll after church this morning; she's moving to Ittibittiwassee Estates."

Lyle asked, "What will happen to Little Mount Vernon?"

Lisa said, "Let's hope she'll leave it to the town for a historical museum."

"I'm sure Alicia wouldn't want it," Mildred said. "She has a career Down Below — in Milwaukee, I think —"

Lyle interrupted, "As Cool Koko would say, '*How ya gonna keep her down on the farm after she's seen Milwaukee?*'"

Mildred went on hesitantly, "Don't mention this, but Alicia travels with a young man — supposed to be her 'driver' because Alicia has some kind of heart problem. Anyway, the idea doesn't set too well with her grandmother."

Lisa said, "I was assistant principal when Alicia came to live with her grandmother, after a family tragedy. She was not only an all-A student, but she came up with good ideas. The school was always trying to raise money for band instruments or a trip to the nation's capital — by selling cookies or Christmas cards. Alicia suggested lotteries, which were very successful, although everyone said she skimmed a little off the top."

Polly said, "That reminds me, she used to bring homework assignments to the library and noticed that we were trying to raise money for new carpet by asking patrons to put money in a jar. Alicia came to me and suggested a lottery, and I told her I'd have to consult the board of directors. When the Dear Ladies learned that it meant gambling, they said, 'Horrors!' and got out their checkbooks to cover the cost of the carpet."

Qwilleran said, "A little horror can be a useful thing!"

"Who said that?" Riker asked. "Ben Franklin or Cool Koko?"

At one point Qwilleran remarked, "I heard, the other day, that the entire wild turkey population of Moose County disappeared thirty years ago. What was that all about?"

70

There was a swift glance between the Comptons, then Lyle said, "Disease. Wiped out the entire flock. It's the kind of thing that happens in the animal world. It'll happen to us if we don't recognize the danger of impure water and polluted atmosphere."

There was a moment's silence until Arch asked, "Who's ready for another drink?"

The subject changed to the grand plans for Brrr's birthday party. Lisa and Mildred were collaborating on a stunt to be called Marmalade Madness.

"You tell it," said Lisa.

"No, it was your idea. You tell it."

"Well . . . Brrr was founded by Scots, you know, and we have a sizable Scottish population. Some of the families have housekeeping manuals, handwritten, that go back as much as two centuries. They keep them in lockboxes at the bank and bring them out for anniversaries. All the books contain tips on making orange marmalade, and — believe me! — there are scores of different theories. Marmalade Madness would combine an exhibit of these artifacts —"

"Under armed guard, I hope," Arch interrupted.

"Absolutely! And the guard will look particularly fierce in kilts and plaids — with antique weapons," Lisa assured him.

"There will also be marmalade-tasting, with people voting for their favorite — all homemade, of course. And the public can buy small jars, proceeds going to charity."

"Where will this be held?" Polly asked.

"Gary Pratt is giving us one of the rooms on the main floor. The ballroom will be used for a variety of happenings, I understand, including Qwill's one-man show."

After brunch, Lyle wanted to walk down to the beach to smoke a cigar, and Qwilleran went along to skip a few stones over the placid water.

"You've got a good pitching arm, Qwill. You missed your calling."

They walked a few yards down the beach. Qwilleran skipped a few more stones and then asked, "When I inquired about wild turkeys, was I getting the whole story?"

"There are some things we don't mention in front of Mildred, but . . . there was a rumor that the wild turkeys were poisoned. Crop farmers and sheep ranchers said they were pests; families objected to the constant gunfire, as hunters knocked off a couple of birds for dinner; and Mildred's first husband, who raised domestic turkeys for the market, said the wild birds were cutting into his profits."

"Was there any investigation about the poisoning?" Qwilleran skipped a few more stones.

"No, the public and officialdom preferred to think the turkeys died of natural causes. You know how they are around here."

As Qwilleran and Polly drove back to Pickax, she said, "The architect is flying up from Chicago tomorrow on the late shuttle. He's asked me to make his hotel reservation for two nights. That will give him one whole day to talk to the builders and work out problems."

Qwilleran asked, "Is your rapport with him strictly business, or is it partly social? In the latter case, I should pick him up at the airport. Otherwise, he can take the airport limousine."

"Let him take the limousine," Polly said. "He does, however, want desperately to see your barn and the Boulder House Inn, both of which he considers architecturally impossible. So, if it's agreeable with you, the builders could drop him off at the barn at the end of the day."

"Do they know where the barn is?"

"Dear, *everyone* knows where your barn is.

You could give him a drink. He likes Scotch. I'll leave the library a little early in order to go home and change clothes. Then you can pick me up at home, and we'll all go to Boulder House Inn."

"Anything you say," he said agreeably, relieved to know that her interest in Benson Hedges — or was it Hodges? — was strictly business.

Chapter Five

For Qwilleran, Tuesday turned out to be an "interesting" day — an adjective he was not prone to use if he could possibly think of a better one.

First, Polly phoned before leaving for the library, reporting briefly that Benson Hodges, the Chicago architect, had checked into the Mackintosh Inn the previous evening and would spend all day conferring with the builders of the bookstore but would have to fly home without having dinner at Boulder House.

"He wants to see your barn, however, and perhaps you can offer him a drink before he catches his shuttle flight."

"I'm not shedding any tears over Benson, Polly. You and I will have dinner at Boulder House. I'll pick you up at the Village at six."

The next caller had the high-pitched

voice of Gary Pratt.

"Hi, Qwill! They're back! Lish and Lush!"

"I'll drive up there with my tape recorder and the old scripts — just to test her skills. The new script — about the Great Storm — should be ready to rehearse in another week."

"I warn you, Qwill! Meeting Lish for the first time is like a plunge into the lake off the end of the hotel dock!"

"I'll wear a wet suit," Qwilleran said.

When he arrived at the Hotel Booze at the appointed hour for the "plunge" he was pleased to see a prize-winning limerick from the "Qwill Pen" column enlarged and framed in the lobby:

> *There was a young lady from Brrr*
> *Who always went swimming in fur.*
> *One day on a dare*
> *She swam in the bare,*
> *And that was the end of her!*

At the appointed hour, Gary introduced Alicia Carroll and the celebrated Mr. Q in a small private dining room on the main floor, concealing his merriment with difficulty. Qwilleran had handed him a slip of paper:

There was a young lady named Lish
Who was said to be cold as a fish.
But with sauce tartare
And some black caviar,
She turned out to be quite a dish!

"Call me Lish," she said in a throaty, husky voice that suggested too much smoking. She had a no-nonsense haircut and no-color pantsuit and a serious but relaxed manner. Her face was basically handsome — with a high brow, high cheekbones, and a firm jaw — but in need of a little makeup.

He opened the tape recorder and handed her a cue sheet. "I sit at a table with a fake mike and the audience hears my newscast live. To introduce other voices and sound effects, you press a button on cue, and the audience hears them over the loudspeaker. It's simple enough, but it requires exquisite timing on your part — to convince the audience that it's real."

She nodded. "Shall we give it a try?"

"You understand," he said, "that this is the show we did last year. There'll be a new script and cue sheet in a few days."

Calmly and precisely Lish pressed the right buttons at exactly the right time, then asked, "Is that all there is to it?"

What could he say? He ignored her question and went on. "There'll be eight shows: the first one on the night of July fourth, the others on alternate Saturday nights in July and August, requiring absolute regularity on your part. This is showbiz," he added lightly.

"No problem," Lish said. "What does it pay?"

Fortunately he had been warned that she was a mercenary type. He said, "The entire two-month spectacle is produced with hundreds of unpaid volunteers, but if you feel you must have remuneration, notify Gary Pratt."

He spoke in a cool, businesslike voice. "If you're interested in a research assignment, I could suggest one that pays the usual hourly rate."

"What is the assignment?" she asked in a detached manner.

"Nothing of vital importance," he replied. "Next time you're in Milwaukee, you might find out whether there is anyone there by the name of Mountclemens or by the name of Bonifield. Also, you might check the catteries listed in the phone book, if anyone specializes in breeding Siamese."

"I could do that. When would you need the information?"

Qwilleran recognized a glint in her eyes, and he chuckled to think, This is a gamble, but . . . no harm in trying. "It's like this," and he explained his curiosity about Kao K'o Kung's antecedents — just enough to capture her interest.

After that, he went home and waited for Gary's phone call.

"How d'you like that greedy little monster? Everyone knows her parents left her a big trust, and she'll inherit from her grandmother!"

"What did you tell her?"

"I told her we have two hundred volunteers working on this celebration for nothing, but we'd be glad to take up a collection from the audience at each performance — to benefit Mr. Qwilleran's assistant. She backed down. But we'd better have an understudy on hand. She could get her revenge by being a no-show."

"Got any ideas, Gary?"

"Tell you what, my wife could handle the job, although she has her hands full with running the marina and organizing the parade of boats. Have you met her, Qwill? Maxine's as smart as they come!"

"Then what's she doing married to you, Gary?" Qwilleran quipped, and the conversation ended in an outburst of friendly jibes.

Qwilleran began work on the script for "The Great Storm." There would have to be a few introductory words of welcome to the audience. Previously, Qwilleran's assistant had done the honors, but both Hixie Rice and Nancy Fincher had been personable young women with pleasing voices. Alicia's classic features were not made for smiling, and her throaty voice, when projected to fill the banquet room, might sound like a croak. In an emergency, Gary himself might extend the welcome, although his high-pitched voice and bearish hulk would surely produce titters in the audience. And Qwilleran still preferred a woman — a young woman.

Then he thought of Gary's wife. He had said she was "sharp," but was she personable? What kind of woman, Qwilleran had often wondered, would marry the eccentric, hairy hotelier — no matter how amiable his personality? The matter would bear investigation.

Meanwhile, he went to work on the script, starting with the welcome to the audience:

Welcome to "The Great Storm of

1913," an original drama written and performed by Jim Qwilleran, based on historical research by Thornton Haggis. You will have to imagine that home radios actually existed in 1913, as you listen to a broadcast covering the worst storm of the century — sinking ships and destroying communities along the shore. The scene is the newsroom of station WPKX in the tower of the county courthouse.

(Room lights black out)

(Stage lights up showing a plain wood table — downstage center — with table mike [fake], upright telephone [disconnected], and a plain wooden chair. At stage right, the studio engineer is seated at the controls. Enter: newscaster wearing heavy mackinaw and heavy boots. He throws script on table, hangs coat over back of chair, tests mike. Music comes from speakers: Gounod's "Waltz" from *Faust*. Music fades out as voice of station announcer comes over speakers.)

This is station WPKX, Pickax, with up-to-the-minute news about a storm caused by three low-pressure systems clashing over the lake. . . . But first a word from our sponsors. . . . Lanspeak Department Store is offering men's all-wool three-piece suits for three dollars, including a free necktie if purchased the first day. Toodle's Grocery has three specials while they last: fresh pineapples, fifteen cents; oranges, ten cents a dozen; and asparagus, two bunches for a quarter. . . . Pickax Garage says, "If you are trading your buggy in on an automobile, order now and take advantage of 1913 prices: a Maxwell touring car for six hundred dollars or a Maxwell runabout for five-fifty. Headlights and windshields included." And now for the news!

That was all Qwilleran had time to write before dressing for dinner. He had to chuckle at the 1913 prices and thought they would amuse the audience. The fifteen-cent pineapple and six-hundred-dollar motorcar were based on actual ads from the *Lockmaster Logger*. Next he would have to wade through Thornton's file of storm news, garnered from historical papers in the public library collection.

All was ready for the visiting architect. Qwilleran had showered and shaved and trimmed his moustache; the cats had been given an early dinner and instruc-

tions as to the proper behavior. Suddenly —
half an hour before schedule — a construc-
tion truck pulled into the barnyard, and a
man in a business suit swung out of the passenger's seat and reached into the cab for a
briefcase and a piece of luggage.

Playing the genial host, Qwilleran stepped
forward with hand extended. "Mr. Hedges,
I presume."

"Hodges," the guest corrected him.
"Can't stay for dinner. Flying out on the
five-thirty. Early meeting in Chicago tomorrow. Can I call a cab from here?"

Qwilleran said, "Come in and have a
drink and see the barn. I'll call a cab."

The architect gazed up at the lofty barn as
if in a trance. "Interesting!" was his final
comment.

"Quite!" said Qwilleran.

"How old?"

"More than a century." Although
Qwilleran usually spoke in whole sentences,
he could be concise, too.

They were being observed by two cats in
the kitchen window.

"Siamese," Hodges said, as if disclosing
an esoteric fact.

"Right! Follow me. You can leave your
luggage on the antique chest at the back
door."

"Safe?" was the typical city dweller's question.

"Absolutely!"

They went around to the rear, which was really the front — with its handsome double doors, eight-sided gazebo, and flowering shrubbery filled with twittering birds.

"Bird garden," Qwilleran pointed out. "Gazebo for the cats."

"Octagonal," said Hodges.

In the foyer, which was as big as a two-car garage, stood a recumbent bicycle as well as a few works of art. "You ride that?" was the question.

"All the time. Drink?"

"Scotch, with a little water."

"Feel free to look around. Good view from the top of the ramp."

Hodges carried his drink around in silence.

"What do you think?" Qwilleran asked when he descended from the third balcony.

"I would have done it a little differently. Who was your architect?"

"Dennis Hough — not registered. Hanged himself from a rafter when the job was finished. . . . Pour again?" Qwilleran tilted the Scotch bottle.

"A little less water this time." Hodges

leaned on the bar. "You like living here?"

"It's not bad."

"Hard to heat?"

"I spend winters in a condo."

"Mrs. Duncan's a nice woman. Ever been married?"

"Once."

"Will a bookstore go over in this town?"

"It should."

A taxi tooted its horn in the barnyard.

Hodges swallowed the last of his Scotch. "How long to reach the airport?"

"No telling! Deer crossings can hold you up. That's why I told the cabdriver to come early."

"Come and see us in Chicago" were his parting words.

"Will do," Qwilleran said.

Once again he was glad for the tape recorder in his pocket. No one would believe the laconic conversation.

A half hour later, Qwilleran picked up Polly for the ride to Boulder House Inn. He remarked, "I thought you said Hedges was interesting."

"Hodges," she corrected him. "Benson knows a lot about everything, but he doesn't say much about anything. You know, dear, I think you have a psychological block about his name, or you're doing it to be mischievous."

He uttered a noncommittal grunt, and Polly enjoyed an amused silence as they drove to the lakeshore.

Boulder House was more than a century old — built of boulders as big as bathtubs, piled one on another without an apparent plan. The dining-room floor was one huge slab of flat stone that had been there forever. There was a resident cat named Rocky, who climbed up the exterior of the building like a mountain goat. And there was a jolly innkeeper, Silas Dingwall, who seemed straight out of a medieval woodcut. He gave Qwilleran and Polly a table in a window overlooking the lake and served them complementary appetizers: two plates of french-fried oysters.

Since Polly was allergic to mollusks, Qwilleran had to consume both servings.

While he chewed, Polly entertained him with salient facts about bookstore design:

"Do you realize that there is a certain psychology in the width of bookstore aisles? If too wide, they destroy the feeling of coziness that is part of the bookstore allure. If too narrow, they make the customer feel jostled and uncomfortable."

Qwilleran murmured something, and she went on:

"I've just learned that impulse purchases account for half of all sales in a small bookstore. That calls for intriguing displays and a chance to pick up books and read the jackets."

After the entrées and the salads, and while they were waiting for dessert, Mr. Dingwall said, "The photographer was here today, taking pictures of the inn for the Brrr souvenir book. We bought four pages."

Polly said, "I hope Rocky was photographed."

"Oh, yes! There's a picture of him peeking into one of the upstairs bedrooms like a naughty Peeping Tom."

"Who was the photographer?" Qwilleran asked.

"Mr. Bushland. A very fine gentleman. And he had a nice young lady helping with the lights."

"He's the best!" Qwilleran said. "He's won national prizes. Rocky may wind up on the cover of a photo magazine."

Later, he said to Polly, "That's the first time I've heard a photographer called a gentleman — and a fine one at that!"

"I wonder who the nice young lady was," she said.

At one point, a waitress hurried from the kitchen and whispered to Mr. Dingwall, who rushed into his office. After that his cheerful manner changed to one of sober concern.

"Is there anything wrong, Mr. Dingwall?" Qwilleran asked.

With a glance at nearby tables, the innkeeper said in a lowered voice, "Plane accident! One of our shuttle flights crashed somewhere in Wisconsin. It was the five-thirty to Chicago. No details."

Polly shuddered and put her face in her hands. "How terrible!" she kept saying.

Qwilleran signaled for the check. "Don't get upset," he told her, "until I phone the paper."

When they were in the car, he called the night editor.

"No one hurt," said the deskman. "It was a forced landing. The pilot brought the plane down in an open field."

To Polly, Qwilleran said, "This will cramp the style of the airport wits and their jokes about Scotch tape and bailing wire."

"What do you suppose Benson will say about it?" she wondered.

"I know that he'll say 'Interesting.' "

Chapter Six

On Wednesdays, the *New York Times* featured a food section, and Qwilleran always walked downtown to buy a copy — not that he wanted to know how to make a Moroccan cheese soufflé. His culinary activity was limited to feeding the cats and making a sandwich for himself. But he liked to read about the great chefs and the important restaurants.

Also, it was a good excuse to drop into the Scottish bakery for scones and marmalade and coffee. "Best marmalade I've ever tasted," he said to the rosy-cheeked woman at the cash register. "Do you make it here?"

"Aye, laddie," she replied. "It's made from my great-grandmother's receipt. It makes a big difference how long you boil the oranges in the sugar water. And how are the wee little kitties, Mr. Q?"

When Qwilleran arrived home with the

newspaper, some cookies, and a jar of homemade marmalade, Koko met him at the door and was all over the place — on and off the kitchen counter, on and off the bar. There seemed to be no reason.

"Why do you think you can throw your weight around, young man?" Qwilleran asked. "You're only a wee little kitty." He had to chuckle.

But Koko was never wrong. There was a message on the answering machine, and the cat seemed to know it was important.

The throaty voice of Lish Carroll was even less attractive when recorded:

"Clarence is driving me to Milwaukee. I will work on your project. Back in time for rehearsals."

Qwilleran was pleased. She had a positive attitude about the show . . . and she might solve the nagging mystery about Koko's background and even his unusual talents. That being the case, what was the cat's antagonism toward Lish? Was it the sound of her voice? Did he remember her pointing finger? Or (and this was ridiculous) did he resent intrusion into his heritage?

"All aboard for the gazebo!" he announced.

It required two trips to transport cats,

coffee, cordless phone, typewriter, and Thornton's thick file of research material. And it would take two hours to select and organize the information and interviews involved.

Applying himself to the task, he faced the formidable challenge of transforming bleak facts into breathtaking radio announcements, starting with Sunday, November 9, 1913.

It was an emotional experience, and he welcomed a respite; he phoned Polly at the library.

"Qwill! I'm glad you called! I've just talked to Benson's office in Chicago. His secretary said he got into Chicago very late last night and had an early meeting this morning, but she said he was none the worse for the forced landing. He told his secretary it was — guess what! — an *interesting* experience. And what about you, Qwill? What have you been doing?"

"Working on my script. I finished segment one, after which the stage lights black out and the audience hears a minute of music. What do you think it should be?"

"*Francesca da Rimini,*" she answered quickly. "It's good storm music."

"We used it for fire music in 'The Big Burning,' " he objected.

"No one will remember, dear."

"I guess you're right."

"*À bientôt!*"

"*À bientôt!*"

What Qwilleran needed now was a writing challenge of a different sort, and he applied himself to *The Private Life of the Cat Who* . . . To date, he had written a dozen sketches, ranging from humorous to scholarly — from Koko's macho exploits to Yum Yum's feminine foibles.

He fortified himself with a cup of coffee and wrote the following:

THE MATTER OF THE SILVER THIMBLE

It's like this: There are thousands of house cats, barn cats, and cat fanciers in Moose County, and readers of my "Qwill Pen" column enjoy hearing about the antics of the Siamese occasionally. They are awed by the handsome, intelligent Koko, but they love the sweet little Yum Yum, with her dainty demeanor and iron will. In fact, there is a Yum Yum fan club in the county.

Members of this unofficial organization send her crocheted mice that squeak and plastic balls that rattle. Her most precious possession, though, is a silver thimble, a gift from a dear reader no longer able to sew. "Cats," she said, "love thimbles."

Yum Yum has always liked anything small and shiny, but she is absolutely infatuated with her thimble.

She bats it around with her delicate paw, carries it from one venue to another in her tiny teeth, hides it, forgets where it's hidden, then cries until I look under rugs, behind seat cushions, and in wastebaskets to retrieve it.

She has deposited it in the pockets of my jackets, in a bowl of mixed nuts, and down the drain of the kitchen sink.

I should take it away from her, but I haven't the heart. She would pine away and die.

I have appealed to readers of the newspaper. All solutions to the problem will be thoughtfully considered. Address me in care of the psychiatric ward at the Pickax General Hospital.

Chapter Seven

The third week in June would be a busy one for Qwilleran, and he felt the need to make a list:

Write "Qwill Pen" for Tuesday. (How about the Toothache Club?)
Write column for Friday. (The Whoozis epidemic.)
Write segment two of script in time for Sunday afternoon rehearsal.
Order daffodils.
Reserve table for Friday night.
Call Bushy about Brrr souvenir book and "nice young lady" working for him.

Not on the list but implicit in Qwilleran's life was the "quality time" he spent with the Siamese twice a week.

No matter how busy Qwilleran might be, nothing was allowed to interfere with the "quality time." He told himself, They're all the family I've got! True, they provided him with companionship, entertainment, and occasional frustration. To Thornton Haggis he had once said, "Anyone who lives alone needs to take responsibility for a fellow creature or risk being blown away."

And Thornton replied, "Your only danger, as I see it, is disappearing in a cloud of hyperbole!"

On this particular morning, the Siamese were treated to a serving of choice red salmon — two servings, his and hers. There followed an interval for catly ablutions, a ritual that only they could understand. Next, they were groomed with their favorite brush — a silver-backed antique that had belonged to the late Iris Cobb.

Then the two males watched patiently while Yum Yum batted her thimble around, hid the thing, forgot where it was, found it, and finally stored it in some secret grotto.

After that, both cats engaged in an athletic romp with a necktie. It always left them exhausted. They flopped over on their sides and lay motionless, except for the tapping of a tail on the floor. This was Qwilleran's cue to nudge a soft underside gently with the toe of a shoe.

Instantly the prostrate cat came to life and attacked Qwilleran's shoe with both forelegs, kicking furiously with hind feet. It was a game they played.

Finally, there was a reading session. Koko, the official bibliocat, sprang to a bookshelf, sniffed bindings, and made a selection. Currently he liked Robert Service poems, apparently for their rollicking rhythms: *I wanted the gold, and I sought it; I scrabbled and mucked like a slave.*

The *Moose County Something* claimed to have ten thousand subscribers, most of whom were members of the Toothache Club, as it was called in the "Qwill Pen" column. They were readers who asked the nagging question: Why do you always get a toothache on a weekend — and it's gone when you get to the dentist's chair on Monday morning? Members added their own unanswered questions and mailed them to the newspaper on postcards. When a sufficient number had accumulated, Qwilleran ran another column on the subject, eagerly awaited by members and nonmembers alike:

"Why does the motorist ahead of you always drive too slow and the one behind you always drive too fast?"

"Did you ever notice that a ten-minute wait standing up is twice as long as a ten-minute wait sitting down?"

"We've all learned that medications have

side effects, but golly if the side effects don't have side effects now!"

Arch Riker kidded the columnist about letting the readers do his work, but actually he liked reader participation. Subscribers talked about the pet peeves in the coffee shops and started mailing in some of their own.

Qwilleran had a pet peeve of his own: He had an intense dislike for unanswered questions. Who was the "nice young lady" helping John Bushland photograph Boulder House for the Brrr souvenir book? He and Roger MacGillivray and Qwilleran had shared a horrendous boating accident that had bonded them for life. The photographer's professional successes and personal tragedies would always concern Qwilleran. Bushy had been unlucky in his choice of assistants, but now a "nice young lady" was assisting him with the lighting on photo jobs. Who was she? Qwilleran called the studio.

"John Bushland Studio. May I help you?" asked a woman's voice that was faintly familiar.

"This is Jim Qwilleran. To whom am I speaking?" he asked with comic formality.

"Qwill! This is Janice Barth! Remember

me from Thelma's house? Remember the parrots . . . the waffles?"

"Of course I do! Especially the waffles. Are you helping Bushy at the studio?"

"Yes, and he's teaching me developing and printing so I can help with the darkroom. Shall I have him call you?"

When the photographer returned the call, Qwilleran said, "My spies tell me you shot the Boulder House for the souvenir book, and you had a 'nice young lady' holding the light."

"Qwill! You nosy devil! You've been snooping again! Well, to make a long story short, Janice is not only on my payroll — we're tying the knot!"

"What? You're marrying her? When? Where?"

"Just a civil ceremony at the house on Pleasant Street, with Roger and his wife as witnesses. After, there'll be a small wedding dinner at the Boulder House Inn, to which you may or may not be invited."

"That being the case, buster, I may or may not pick up the check for the dinner — as a wedding gift to a pal who once tried to drown me. Meanwhile, someone should warn Janice that you're just looking for free darkroom service. How about the five par-

98

rots? Do you have to support them?"

And so it went. Before Qwilleran could return to work on "The Great Storm," he had a brilliant idea! He called his friend Simmons in California. The retired police detective had been a security officer at Thelma Thackeray's dinner club, gradually becoming a friend of the family with a standing invitation to Sunday-morning waffles. To Janice he was a kindly uncle. And when Thelma had sent him a plane ticket to Pickax, Simmons and Qwilleran had struck an immediate rapport — the retired cop and the former crime reporter. Now Qwilleran would send him a plane ticket, and Simmons would be the surprise guest at the wedding dinner. Janice would be overcome with delight.

Qwilleran tracked Simmons down at his daughter's house, where he was babysitting his grandchildren. He said, "Sounds great! But I have a security job lined up for July fourth that's too good to pass up. Tell you what I could do: take the red-eye flight to Chicago and then the morning shuttle flight to Moose County. Thanks for thinking of me, Qwill. I'm very happy for Janice."

Qwilleran said, "Also, you'll be interested to know that a dead body was found on my property at the beach, and police are investigating. And investigating. And investigating. Perhaps you and I can solve the case."

As the week wore on, Qwilleran worked on the second segment of the "Great Storm" script and wrote a "Qwill Pen" column for Friday, decrying the increase in bad manners among phone users. He blamed people in a perpetual hurry, people phoning from their cars, and telephone subscribers annoyed by calls from salespersons and solicitors. Too many persons were shouting "Who's this?" into the mouthpiece . . . or "Whoozis?" The offending party could be the one answering the phone, or a caller who has reached a wrong number, or anyone too busy to care about civilities.

Qwilleran wrote, "Is this a fad? A phenomenon? A social disease, peculiar to areas 400 miles north of everywhere? If you are a member of the Whoozis Club, please drop us a postal card. The 'Qwill Pen' would like to be enlightened."

Friday, June 20, had been circled on Qwilleran's calendar. It was his mother's birthday! She had died when he was in college, and after that his life had been a roller-coaster ride.

Then, suddenly, Anne Mackintosh Qwilleran came rushing back into his memory again. He had read letters she had written to a friend before he was born. They were the key that unlocked the door to his early life. She was a single parent. His father had died before Qwilleran was born. Now he could appreciate her efforts to give him a normal upbringing.

Jamie, she called him. He had a playmate called Archie, whose dad took the two boys to the zoo, parades, and ball games. As the boys grew older, Mr. Riker gave them the advice needed from a father.

There were certain things Qwilleran remembered about Lady Anne, as he now called her: how she always recited the same poem on her birthday . . . how her fingers flew when she played "Flight of the Bumblebee" on the piano, and how she always wore a bracelet with dangling coins.

Now Arch Riker was back in his life, as editor-in-chief of the newspaper, and it seemed only fitting that he and Mildred and Polly should honor Lady Anne on her birthday.

At the end of the workday, the foursome gathered at the barn and drank a toast to Lady Anne. Then Polly read the Wordsworth poem — the one that began:

101

I wandered lonely as a cloud
That floats on high o'er vales and hills,
When all at once I saw a crowd,
A host, of golden daffodils.

The "Qwill Pen" had promoted the idea that everyone should have a birthday poem. Qwilleran himself had adopted Kipling as his birthday poet: "If you can keep your head when all about you are losing theirs and blaming it on you . . ."

Wetherby Goode, the WPKX meteorologist, had chosen Carl Sandburg: "The fog comes on little cat feet . . ."

Mildred, who had survived more than her share of personal tragedies, quoted Lizette Woodworth Reese: "When I consider life and its few years . . . I wonder at the idleness of tears . . ."

Polly quoted Wordsworth, although she said she had to change a word here and there: "My heart leaps up when I behold a rainbow in the sky . . ."

Arch quoted Anonymous: "I know two things about a horse, and one of them is rather coarse."

Then the host rushed his guests off to the Old Grist Mill, where two champagne buckets crowded with daffodils stood on a console table in the foyer. A card read: In memory of Anne Mackintosh Qwilleran.

Mildred asked, "How did you round up so many flowers — without baby's breath or ribbon bows or other additives?"

"The daffodils were ordered from Chicago," Qwilleran said, "and I told the florist to send them directly to the restaurant, because they were being used in a salad."

Riker said, "Qwill was always a master of creative fibbing."

That said, they drank a solemn toast to the memory of "Lady Anne."

Then they discussed the Brrr birthday party: Five hundred pages had been purchased in the souvenir book. Twenty thousand T-shirts had been ordered — with the same logo being used on the official poster: "Brrr" and "200" in red on a white background, surrounded by a blue lifesaver. John Bushland was getting married again, and they'd live in Thelma's house. Polly quoted book-selling statistics that related sales potential to square footage, and Qwilleran said that the script of "The Great Storm" would be ready for rehearsal Sunday afternoon — even if he had to stay up all night Saturday.

 The week was not over. On Saturday, Qwilleran finished part two of the "Great Storm" script, and when

Thornton phoned from the Art Center, he was invited to walk up the lane and listen to a run-through.

Qwilleran, besides reading and emoting, had to press the buttons that brought in the voices of eyewitnesses, so the timing was not as crisp as it would be onstage. Even so, Thornton found the show gripping and absolutely real. Qwilleran protested modestly, but actually . . . he thought so, too.

He and Polly agreed to forgo their usual Saturday-night date — she to study the psychology of a bookstore's floor plan, and Qwilleran to psych himself up for the rehearsal the next afternoon.

Then, on Sunday morning, Gary Pratt phoned, his high-pitched voice reaching new heights of emotion:

"Qwill! You'll never guess what! Lish just called. She's still in Milwaukee! Can't be here for rehearsal! Isn't that a beast! She said she was doing some research for you down there, and it was taking longer than she expected. Is that true?"

"Basically, but it was a minor assignment and not worth missing a rehearsal."

"She said to tell you she has some hot news for you."

Qwilleran grunted noncommittally.

"Are you going to be up this way, Qwill? I

need to talk and get something off my chest. Maxine said I should talk to you."

"Any trouble?" Qwilleran asked.

"Well . . . yes and no."

Unanswered questions were anathema to Qwilleran, and he found himself hungering for a bear burger, Hotel Booze style. On arrival, "You look like a sick bear," he told Gary.

"I didn't sleep a wink last night," Gary said. "I got to worrying about something Lish said when she and Lush were hanging around the bar: Someday Mount Vernon would be hers, and she was gonna make it into a bed-and-breakfast and build condos on the back of the property. I didn't think anything of it at the time; people like to talk big at bars. But last night I thought, Hey! Maybe she means it! There's a story, you know, about a barfly who boasted he was gonna blow up city hall, and no one believed him."

"But he blew it up!" Qwilleran said. "It's a classic situation."

"Yeah, and now that her grandmother has taken an apartment at the retirement center so she can have assisted care, when and if! Maybe she doesn't have long to live! Maybe Lish can carry out her boast! My stomach turns over at the thought of that historic house going commercial! That beautiful house! It's been called the jewel in the crown of the Brrr Parkway. Great spot for a B and B, right?" he added bitterly. "The thing of it is, I never liked Lish in school. She was stuck-up! She had her own car and a special permit for underage driving. She got all A's. The only thing she didn't get was . . . dates! The guys couldn't stand her!"

"Why did you recommend her, Gary, for the show?"

"Well, y'see, I wanted to show her what kind of things we do here now, and what kind of people are living here. We're not a bunch of hicks."

Cheerfully, Qwilleran said, "It looks as if you're up a creek without a paddle, friend, but there's a solution to every problem. All it takes is a little thought. Any idea when Lish and Lush will return?"

"Maybe her grandmother does. Wonder what the old gal thinks of Lush. You just know she wants Lish to marry a doctor, and settle down, and raise a family, and be president of the PTA, and sing in the church choir! It's funny! So why ain't I laughing?"

Chapter Eight

Qwilleran had ambivalent reactions to the canceled rehearsal. He had worked hard to meet the deadline. And yet — if it meant the answer to the long-unanswered question about Koko's background — he would call it an even exchange. Only someone who has lived for years with a psychic cat could understand his attitude.

On Sunday morning he phoned Polly, although he was sure she would be attending church services. He left a message: "Rehearsal postponed. Taking cats to the beach. Will call you tonight. *À bientôt.*"

Next he grabbed Yum Yum before she knew what was happening and pushed her, protesting, into the travel coop. Koko entered it willingly. Then Qwilleran filled a picnic basket with cold drinks in an ice pack, a ham sandwich for himself, crunchies for the Siamese, and two molasses-ginger cookies from the Scottish bakery. He wondered how these plain, flat, brown cookies could be so humble and yet so delectable. Upon further consideration, he put all four in the basket.

It was only a half-hour drive from the grandiose barn to the snug, friendly log cabin. On arrival the three of them trooped to the screened porch overlooking the lake.

It was a beautiful day. The water splashed gently on the shore. Sandpipers ran up and down like wind-up toys. A soft breeze wafted the tall beach grass that covered the side of the dune. And there was always one tiny bird, weighing a tenth of an ounce, perched on the tip of a blade of grass and riding back and forth.

Koko immediately assumed his Egyptian-cat pose on the tall pedestal that he considered his own. Yum Yum ran around, batting insects on the outside of the screen. Qwilleran lounged in a chair and propped his feet on a footstool.

After a while Koko emitted a throaty rumbling and pointed his ears to the east. In a few moments a pair of beach walkers approached, looking for agates and dropping them in a small plastic sack.

Qwilleran went out to the top of the sand-ladder and shouted, "Would you two trespassers like to come up for a cold drink?"

Lisa and Lyle Compton, both wearing "BRRR 200" T-shirts, gladly accepted.

They sat on the porch, and Qwilleran served Squunk water with a dash of cranberry juice. The Siamese were comfortable with the Comptons and paid them the compliment of ignoring them — Yum Yum batting her bugs, Koko preening himself all over.

Lyle said, "I'm looking forward to seeing your show on the Great Storm. My elders lived through it but weren't inclined to talk about it. They had the pioneer tendency to make light of hardships, even telling jokes about unfortunate happenings."

Lisa agreed. "My grandfather lived through the Great Storm. On the stormiest night, the high winds destroyed his chicken coop and sent a board sailing through the kitchen window. The family was asleep upstairs and didn't know about it until morning, when they went downstairs and found all the chickens in the kitchen, roosting on the nice, warm stovepipe."

Lyle said, "And then there's the story that everyone tells about a couple of fellows named Alf Kirby and Bill Durby, who worked for the railroad as fireman and brakeman. Two or three nights a week they had to sleep over, and the company let them use a two-room cottage between the tracks and the lakefront. Durby, having seniority, had the room overlooking the lake — the only trouble being that the lake breezes rattled the windows on a cold night and there was frost on the ceiling in the morning. On the night of the Great Storm, Durby offered Kirby five dollars to exchange rooms, and Kirby agreed, always interested in a good deal. But the winds were of gale force on that night, and they turned the little cottage around on its foundation, so that Durby was still on the cold side minus five bucks."

"Yow!" came a strong reaction from Koko on his pedestal.

"What does that mean?" Lyle demanded.

"Koko thinks it's a good tale, but he doesn't believe a word of it. I'd like to know about Scottish Night at the Brrr celebration."

Lisa, whose maiden name was Campbell, and Lyle, whose mother was a Ross, were eager to report the details: It would be a preview of the two-month celebration. All the clans would be there in Highland attire. The park across from the hotel would be strung with Japanese lanterns — festive in daylight, magical after dark. In the bandstand, bagpipers would pipe, dancers would do the Highland Fling, and a Scottish quartet would sing tearjerkers. And Miss Agatha Burns would throw the switch to light the ten-foot birthday cake with its two hundred electric candles.

"Should I know her?" Qwilleran asked. He was quickly informed that she was a retired teacher, a hundred years old, now confined to a wheelchair and living at the Senior Care Facility.

Lisa said, "Three generations of students have annually voted Miss Agatha their favorite teacher. She had charisma. She made us want to learn."

Qwilleran asked, "What did she teach?"

Lyle said with unusual fervor, "What the State Board of Ed called dead languages! Can you believe that my father had four years of Latin and a year of classical Greek — here in the boondocks? The state made us eliminate those two subjects, consolidate with Pickax High School, and buy a fleet of school buses that would pollute the atmosphere! Kids used to walk two or three miles to school and thought nothing of it."

Qwilleran asked, "What did she teach after that?"

"English," said Lisa, "but she taught us the Latin roots of English words."

"Would a 'Qwill Pen' column on Miss Agatha be a good idea to coincide with the opening of Brrr Two hundred?"

"Perfect!" said Lyle. "But she's had a stroke and doesn't speak. It would be better to interview her former students. There are plenty of them in the Old-Timers Club and at Ittibittiwassee Estates."

"Would Alicia's grandmother be one of them?"

"She's quite reserved," Lisa said. "She wouldn't be easy to interview."

That was no obstacle to a veteran columnist.

He had a talent for winning confidences from the most reticent subjects. His rich, mellow voice made them feel good. He listened attentively, nodded sympathetically, and gazed at them with a brooding expression that won their trust.

He asked, "Have you ever been in the Carrolls' house?"

"Once," Lisa said. "She never did much entertaining, but this was a tea for a church benefit. It's a beautiful house, filled with American and English antiques: Chippendale, Newport, Duncan Phyfe, Queen Anne — you name it!"

Lyle said, "If she has a sentimental notion that her granddaughter will leave Milwaukee and live in it, she's dotty. Alicia will sell the antiques to a New York dealer and

112

the house to a developer, who'll carve it into apartments and build condos on the grounds."

"Yow!" came an imperious interruption from the pedestal.

The guests stood up. "He's telling us to go home."

Qwilleran had an idea, and he was in a hurry to put it into action. Back at the barn, he inscribed a copy of *Short & Tall Tales* to Dr. Wendell Carroll, Dr. Hector Carroll, and Dr. Erasmus Carroll — the three generations of medics who had served Moose County since pioneer days. He enclosed a note — and his unlisted phone number. This he clipped to the legend titled "Housecalls on Horseback" and then had the book delivered by motorcycle messenger to Ittibittiwassee Estates.

It was not long before the phone rang, and a sweet, cultivated voice said, "Mr. Qwilleran, this is Edythe Carroll. We have never met, and I am deeply touched that you should send me this splendid book. The account of the pioneer doctors is so true! It might have been handed down from Dr. Erasmus!"

For one who was considered reticent and aloof, Mrs. Carroll was remarkably talkative. Qwilleran murmured the right things.

"And you mentioned in your note, Mr. Qwilleran, that you have an idea you wish to discuss. Would you do me the honor of taking tea with me tomorrow?"

Qwilleran trimmed his moustache, dressed properly for tea with Dr. Wendell's widow, and drove to the retirement village.

She received him graciously in an apartment that was clearly furnished with her own heirlooms. She had white hair, attractively styled for her age, and she wore a lavender silk dress and a little color on her cheeks.

"Do you like antiques?" she asked as she ushered Qwilleran into the small sitting room.

"I admire the design and fine woods of individual pieces," he replied frankly, "but most people crowd too many into a given space. You handle them with great taste."

"Thank you," she said with obvious delight. "My late husband disliked clutter, too."

He had caught a glimpse, as he passed a china cabinet, of a number of small decorated china objects, like saltcellars. On second glance, they proved to be miniature shoes.

He stopped and said, "This is a remarkable collection! I've never seen anything like it!"

"Miniature porcelain shoes are quite collectible," she said, "and my husband and I had a romantic interest in collecting, but I won't bore you with that! Come and sit at the tea table, and I'll bring the tea."

When she appeared at the kitchen door with a loaded tray, Qwilleran jumped up and carried it to the table. Older women always liked Qwilleran's courtly manners, which he had learned "at his mother's knee," he liked to say. He knew very well they would make a positive impression on Lish's grandmother.

They sat at a Queen Anne tea table, and Mrs. Carroll poured tea into thin porcelain cups. "This is Darjeeling," she said, "best with a little warm milk." She raised the silver cream pitcher tentatively.

He said, "Please."

At that point Qwilleran inquired, "Do you feel inclined to tell me the romantic story about your collection of shoes? I assure you I would never be bored."

"You promise?" she cried, eager to tell all.

"When I was a young woman, I attended the Lockmaster Academy and studied ballet. One of our recitals was attended by a group of young men, including Dr. Wendell Carroll, who was specializing in foot surgery. He said later that he fell in love with my tiny feet. We were eventually married and started a collection of miniature shoes. Whenever Dell returned from a medical conference in Chicago or another big city, he'd burst into the house shouting: *Edie! I found another shoe!*"

She cast a wistful glance at the china cabinet. They sat in thoughtful silence for a moment or two. Then Qwilleran asked, "Did you ever know a teacher named Agatha Burns? She's a hundred years old, and I'm writing a column about her."

"Yes, indeed! She was an inspiration! She even encouraged me to write poems in Latin, and one of them won a prize! Fifteen dollars! I bought a typewriter with it — secondhand manual. I still have it! I suppose you use a computer."

"No, I use a vintage electric typewriter that reads my mind and knows what key I'm going to press next. But there's nothing like an old manual with its clattering keys, loud bells, and the authoritative thump when the carriage returns."

She appreciated the humor and swayed with mirth.

"May I call you Edythe? It's a name with a pleasant sound."

"Please do," she said.

"Edythe, have you ever thought of presenting Mount Vernon to the community as a memorial to the three Carroll doctors — together with your exquisite antiques — to be admired and revered as a museum?"

Tears welled into her eyes, and she dabbed them with a handkerchief — a real one, with lace trimming. "Oh, I don't know what to say!" she cried. "I'm overcome with emotion at your kind suggestion. You don't know what it would mean to me, Mr. Qwilleran."

"Please call me Qwill," he said in the mellifluous voice that had worked miracles in the past. "I'm not aware of your plans for the house, but whatever they are, I wish you would consider honoring three generations of medical men in this way.

"Your antiques would be admired by visitors from all over the United States. One room could be set aside for the pioneer doctors and their primitive medical equipment: the saws they used for amputations without anesthesia . . . the medicines they mixed themselves . . . the folding operating table carried in the doctor's buggy for surgery in the patient's kitchen. The county historical society has plenty of such relics that they could lend, including what must be the world's largest collection of bedpans!"

Overlooking the whimsical exaggeration, Mrs. Carroll said abruptly, "My granddaughter is expecting to inherit the house."

"Would she be willing to share it with the community?" He knew it was an absurd question.

"I'm afraid not. She'll sell it to the highest bidder to make money — for whatever purpose. She sees it as a mall or amusement park, although I'm sure she says it simply to horrify me."

"Has your will been written?"

"It's at the law office, being revised." She bit her lip before saying, "Alicia and her driver are out of town, and I went to the house to check its condition. I was appalled! There were food containers on my lovely mahogany dining table . . . soiled clothing on the Orientals . . . and garbage in the kitchen sink. Alicia was never very tidy in her ways, but this! It must be her . . . driver! I don't know what to do!"

"May I make a suggestion, Edythe?"

The sound of her first name brought her to attention.

"Of course!"

"Call your attorney without delay! He might advise hiring a caretaker . . . changing the locks on the doors . . . and swift action on a revised will. Tell him you want it to be the Carroll Memorial Museum. There's nothing of the sort in the whole county!" He stopped suddenly, remembering the dashed plans for a Klingenschoen Museum. Then he said with less vehemence, "Was Mount Vernon your idea?"

"My father-in-law's. He was a great admirer of George Washington."

"All the more reason why you should preserve it. Don't wait till it's too late."

As Qwilleran drove away from Mrs. Carroll's apartment in Ittibittiwassee Estates, he had a great feeling of satisfaction. One thing had to be made clear: He wanted to stay out of the picture.

That evening when he and Polly had their nightly phone chat, she said, "It was a quiet day at the library. What did you do, dear?"

"Worked on my Tuesday column. Have you been doing your homework?"

"Yes. Do you realize the importance of aisle width in a bookstore? Physically and

119

psychologically! There must be plenty of room for customers and staff to move around. It's good for a bookstore to be crowded at times, but not too crowded so that individual customers feel jostled."

"I see," Qwilleran said. "Quite an absorbing subject."

"But I'm taking an evening off for the bird club," she said. "The speaker is an expert on the tufted titmouse."

"Is that a bird?" he asked slyly.

"An adorable little bird — with yellow breast."

"Strange name for a bird. Why is it called a titmouse?"

"Would you like to attend the meeting — and bring up the subject?"

"Maybe I will. What are they having for dinner? Chicken potpie again?"

It was the easy rambling of two close friends who talk to each other on the phone every evening.

"*À bientôt*," she said.

"*À bientôt*."

Chapter Nine

As Qwilleran was leaving the barn Tuesday morning, he was accompanied to the exit by the Siamese, who sat on their haunches and awaited his farewell as if they knew what he was saying. He always told them where he was going, what he would be doing, and when he would return. After he left, they would race around the barn, whisking papers off the desk and overturning wastebaskets. As Cool Koko would say, *When the man's away, the cats will play.*

Qwilleran drove to the town of Brrr, which he knew only for its superlative burgers at the Black Bear Café in the Hotel Booze. For the first time he noticed the small park across the street, with its modest fountain and uncomfortable benches on which no one cared to sit.

His curiosity aroused, Qwilleran drove around town and saw a thriving business district . . . a monument to the Scots who founded the town . . . a fringe of residential streets . . . and the broad avenue known as the Parkway. It was lined with stone residences of impressive size, built in the nineteenth century, and at the very end, gleaming like a beacon in the sunlight, was the white frame replica of Mount Vernon, built by the second Dr. Carroll. It had the red roof and broad lawns of the original, but the grass needed cutting.

Qwilleran's real reason for visiting Brrr was to meet Maxine Pratt, who would now handle the sound effects for the show. He drove down a side street that circled the hotel and sloped down to the harbor. On the boardwalk a young woman in yachting cap and royal-blue jumpsuit was giving orders to a young blond giant grasping a hammer. He nodded as she pointed and explained, and then he trotted down the pier to fix loose boards.

The woman turned and saw the famous moustache. "Qwill!" she cried.

"Are you Gary's wife," he asked, "or are you wearing her jumpsuit?" The name "Maxine" was embroidered on the breast pocket.

"Gary has told me so much about you!"

"Why is a nice woman like you married to that hairy brute?"

"He may look like a black bear, but he's a real pussycat," she said. "We used to go out in his sailboat, and he'd talk about how a sky full of sail and a whispering breeze can touch the soul of a man. And I knew he couldn't be all bad."

"I'm glad you got together," Qwilleran said. "Now when can you and I get together for a technical rehearsal? All we need is a quiet room with two tables and two chairs."

"Tomorrow night, about eight o'clock?" she suggested.

"Perfect! I've brought you a cue card and also a copy of the script, so you can see what happens between cues."

"You're so well organized, Qwill!"

"It's a lot easier than organizing a parade of two hundred boats. How will it work? Will they parade single file?"

"No, in fleets of about twenty-five. There are eight towns on the lakefront, and each will have a fleet — and a port master in charge."

Qwilleran noticed some eager-looking tourists coming along the boardwalk, and he said, "Tell me the rest of it tomorrow night. Bring the speech you'll be making to the audience."

"I've memorized it already!" she said proudly.

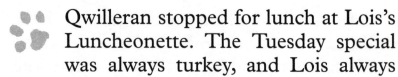 Qwilleran stopped for lunch at Lois's Luncheonette. The Tuesday special was always turkey, and Lois always sent a few pieces of meat home to the Siamese. Then he went to the barn for a private run-through of the script.

Now he had to decide how much emotion to put in his voice as a broadcaster. How objective should he be in reporting the first bulletins? And how much concern should he show as the bulletins went from bad to worse? His tone of voice, as well as the words he was reading, would increase the reactions of the audience. When satisfied with the dramatic effect created and the sense of reality maintained, Qwilleran had a cup of coffee and then did another run-through, pressing the PLAY button to bring in the eyewitness reports. So far, so good, but with an assistant handling the controls, the pace would quicken and the emotions of the audience would intensify.

Despite the assorted noises, the Siamese slept peacefully on their cushioned chair . . . until an inaudible sound jerked both of them awake and started their ears swiveling. It could only mean that someone was coming! Qwilleran left the gazebo and walked around the building to the barnyard in time to see a car emerging from the woods, purring like a well-tuned vehicle. The cats could not have heard someone coming; they had sensed it in their sleep. Qwilleran shook his head; it was too much to fathom.

At any rate, he was glad to see his friend G. Allen Barter from the law office. "Bart! What brings you sneaking through the woods like a poacher? How about a drink?"

"Not today, thanks. I'm on my way home, but I was at the courthouse and decided it would be easier to drop in than to call on this erratic cell phone."

They went to the gazebo, and the attorney spoke to the Siamese, who responded by going back to sleep. He said, "Beautiful day! Did I interrupt something?"

"Not at all. Have a chair — I warn you, they all have cat hairs on them — and tell me what's on your mind."

"Well, our senior partner received a panicked call from an important client. She said that you, Qwill, had advised her to disinherit her granddaughter, evict her from the house on the Parkway, change the locks, and hire a security guard!"

Calmly, Qwilleran replied, "I advised her to hire a housekeeper, but I suppose a security guard can cut the grass, too."

"Also, she said that you, Qwill, told her to

donate the property to the community for a museum."

"Is that all?"

"Isn't that enough? How did you get involved with Dr. Carroll's widow? I'm interested only in you as my client. My partner seemed to think everything made sense."

Then Bart asked, "Does anyone know when the young people will be back from . . . wherever they've gone?"

"Milwaukee — on business. I hired Alicia to do some research for me while she was there, so I'm sure she'll report to me — to collect her fee, if for no other reason."

"Has she been here to the barn?"

"No. Gary is particular about not giving out my phone number and address. It's his idea, not my request, but I appreciate it."

Barter nodded. "He's an all-right guy, with a lot of common sense. . . . So why does he have to wear that ridiculous beard?"

"He's descended from pioneers, and they were — and still are — individualists. Although I must say that he shaved it off for his wedding, and everyone said he looked like a nonentity."

"And, by the way, there's a curious sidelight to this domestic drama," Bart said. "I'm a greenhorn from Down Below, and it amazes me how the locals descend on their relatives without warning and stay overnight. The element of surprise appears to be part of the fun. They may bring their sleeping bags and bed down on the living room carpet; the sleeping bags are another part of the fun. . . . Well, Mrs. Carroll tells us that her granddaughter always drops in without warning. Suppose the girl turns up on the holiday weekend and finds herself locked out of Mount Vernon, and Ittibittiwassee Estates takes a dim view of unwedded couples camping on the living-room carpet; and every tourist accommodation is booked solid. The two letters sent to Alicia each contained a list of accommodations with a sold-out notice. But what if the young couple come right here from wherever they are without touching base in Milwaukee! Then what?"

"Don't look at me," Qwilleran said. "My guest room is not available. And I think the cats don't care for Alicia; they've never met her, but Koko snarls every time she talks on the phone." He refrained from mentioning the nature of the assignment he had given her. Qwilleran himself was beginning to consider the research a lost cause.

A moment later, an ear-shattering, blood-curdling howl came from the corner of the gazebo.

The attorney jumped to his feet. "What the devil was that?"

Qwilleran said, "Just something that Siamese males do to attract attention."

"Sounds to me as if he has a bellyache. Better give him a pill! . . . Well, since I'm on my feet, I might as well go home."

Bart left, and Qwilleran gave Koko a searching look. That unsettling howl had nothing to do with indigestion. It meant that someone, somewhere, had been murdered, and there was significance to the crime. As for Qwilleran, he was still experiencing the goose bumps caused by Koko's howl, and he rubbed both arms to restore the circulation.

Qwilleran treated himself to a solitary dinner at the Black Bear Café before the technical rehearsal with Maxine. By sitting at the bar, he could exchange a few words with Gary, as he shuffled back and forth, filling drink orders.

On this occasion the barkeeper was acting in a most unusual way: saying nothing, glancing about as if he expected to be raided, and altogether exuding an air of mystery.

Finally, Qwilleran said, "Is there something you want to tell me, Gary? Don't tell me the Pratts are pregnant!"

Ignoring the quip, Gary wiped the top of the bar at length before confiding in a low voice, "Just heard the most spectacular rumor."

"Are you keeping it to yourself, or do you want to tell me?"

"Promise you won't tell a soul!"

"Promise!" As a journalist, Qwilleran could never tolerate not knowing.

Gary gave two swift looks up and down the bar. "Brrr is getting Mount Vernon, complete with antiques, as a museum!"

"No kidding! Where did you hear it?"

"I've sworn not to tell. But it'll be front-page news in the *Something* soon."

"It would be interesting to know who engineered the deal, wouldn't it, Gary?"

"Yeah . . . well . . . we'll never know. What I'd like to know is how it'll affect Lish and Lush; they've been campin' out at the house, y'know." Then he was called away to pour a tray full of drinks for a waitress, and that was the end of grand intrigue for that evening.

Qwilleran was still enjoying a private chuckle when he met Maxine in a small room off the foyer. She was much too businesslike to have heard the rumor. "Okay! How do we do this?" she asked, clapping her hands together. "I'm all excited!"

"You at your recorder, Maxine, and I at my mike will both be facing the audience. First, I'd like to hear your introduction to them. You'll walk to the front of the platform and face the crowd to make your speech, then immediately return to your machine and press the first button. You sit down and stay seated until we take our bow at the end."

"Is there an intermission?"

"Not for the audience and not for you, but I leave the stage to denote the passage of time — during which your recorder is playing *storm music.*"

"What kind of expression should I wear?"

"Alert. Concerned. No reaction to the news, though."

"And what should I wear?"

"Something ageless and timeless, like a blouse and skirt, so long as the blouse has a high neck and the skirt isn't too much above the ankles. You should wear it a week from tonight, for our dress rehearsal."

Maxine was so efficient, so agreeable, that Qwilleran contemplated doing more than the scheduled seven performances.

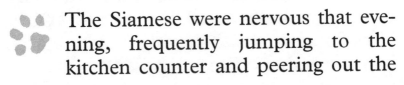 The Siamese were nervous that evening, frequently jumping to the kitchen counter and peering out the

window into the darkness of the woods.

"Expecting someone?" Qwilleran asked archly.

Eventually a vehicle came swooping through the trees and stopped at the kitchen door with the assurance of a frequent visitor. The cats started frisking around — their body language for *Here he is!*

"What brings you here in such a cloud of dust?" Qwilleran asked.

"Thirsty, mon!" said Chief Brodie, "and some fresh-breaking police news."

He seated himself at the snack bar, and Qwilleran served Scotch and cheese, and the cats observed from a respectful distance.

"Don't keep me in suspense, Andy. Have they caught the vandal who's been soaping windows?" Qwilleran asked facetiously.

Dismissing the weak quip with a grunt, Brodie said, "There's been a copycat murder in northern Michigan — like the one on your property — same MO . . . same type of weapon . . . same sort of victim . . . same sort of wooded terrain."

"Do similarities like that aid in the investigation?" Qwilleran asked absently. His mind was elsewhere. He was thinking of Koko's death howl. It was not the first time that the remarkable cat had sensed wrongdoing in some distant spot.

No matter how remote, there was always a connection to the here and now. That was the reason Qwilleran had wanted to investigate Koko's heritage.

Chapter Ten

 It was panic time in the octagonal barn on Saturday night — although not for the two cats huddled atop the fireplace cube, gazing down on the frantic scene below. Four humans were scrambling about on hands and knees, rolling up rugs, climbing a stepladder, pulling seat cushions off the upholstered furniture, dumping wastebaskets on the floor.

"Here it is! I've found it!" cried Mildred Riker.

"Thank God! I thought she'd swallowed it!" Qwilleran shouted.

"You should keep it in a locked drawer," Arch Riker suggested with authority.

Polly Duncan — assuming the voice of the WPKX gossip reporter — said, "A mad thimble scramble was held at the James Mackintosh Qwilleran residence Saturday night. Refreshments were served, and everyone had a good time."

"Make mine a double martini," said Arch.

Qwilleran poured dry sherry for Polly and mixed Q cocktails for Mildred and himself. Then they sat around the big square cocktail table with bowls of peanuts in red skins.

Arch said, "I don't like the skins."

"They're nutritious, hon," his wife said.

"I don't like anything that's good for me."

"He's just trying to sound macho," she explained.

The four of them were old friends, and the rule of conversation was: Anything goes. The two men had been friends since kindergarten in Chicago.

Qwilleran asked, "Do you ever hear from your sister, Arch?"

"Oh, sure. She's living with her second husband in Kansas and selling real estate and still writing in her diary."

Mildred said, "Did I detect a snicker from both of you?"

Qwilleran said, "We might as well confess, Arch. We stole her diary once."

"We only borrowed it from her dresser drawer while she was ice-skating. We were in fifth grade; she was in seventh and getting interested in boys."

"It was hot stuff!" Qwilleran said. "She used code names to refer to different boys. How *George Washington* looked at her in a strange way and made her feel weak all over. And *Benjamin Franklin* said, 'Hi!' in history class, and she almost fainted."

Arch said, "We returned the diary carefully, but she had set a trap for us, and the jig was up! It was all his idea!" Arch pointed a finger at his old friend. "But I was the one who got punished. I lost a week's allowance."

"As I recall," Qwilleran said, "I very nobly gave you half of mine."

"Yeah, but I also had to give up desserts for three nights, while she sat across the dinner table, grinning like a fiend!"

Mildred and Polly glanced at each other and rolled their eyes in resignation.

At that point, Yum Yum walked among them, carrying her thimble clamped in her jaws, and the question arose: Why do cats like thimbles? (They're small and can be hidden; they're round and can be rolled.)

Qwilleran said, "Let's take a vote: Have another round of drinks or go to dinner?"

Arch lost, and they drove to the Nutcracker Inn on the bank of Black Creek. It occupied a Victorian mansion famous for its black walnut paneling and its roast loin of pork. They ordered the house specialty all around. The food was superb; conversation flowed easily; the squirrels in the yard entertained with their antics; the chef came out from the kitchen and kissed the ladies' hands. Everything went well until . . .

In the middle of the night Qwilleran had a nightmare; Lish and Lush moved into his guest suite on the second balcony, despite Koko's snarls. The dream was so real and so objectionable that Qwilleran had to get a flashlight and walk three times around the barn in his pajamas, disturbing the creatures of the night who scuttled through the underbrush and fluttered in the trees.

When he finally came indoors, Qwilleran wrote in his personal journal before going back to bed.

Saturday, June 28. Correction — Sunday morning, June 29:

Why did I order pork for dinner? Why did I ever consider that mercenary prima donna for my Great Storm show? And why did I commission her to do research — and give her fifty dollars on faith? It's pure conceit on my part to want to know Koko's background. As for that smart cat, he doesn't care a whit whether he's descended from a royal household in ancient Siam or from a computer, as long as he gets two squares a day, a couple of snacks, grooming with a silver-backed brush, and plenty of entertainment!

The call from California came around noon on Monday, reporting the arrival time of Simmons's flight the following Saturday.

"Good! I'll pick you up at the airport," Qwilleran said. "We'll drop your luggage at the barn, and you'll have time to change into something for the wedding dinner."

"Any suggestions for a wedding present?"

"Not a waffle iron!" Qwilleran winced at the roar of laughter in his ear. "They'll be living in Thelma's house, which is completely furnished and equipped, as you know."

"Something else, Qwill. When I worked in Thelma's dinner club as a security guard disguised as a friendly host, some peculiar things happened, and I jotted them down in a notebook. I don't pretend to be a writer, and it's just a school notebook, but I thought of wrapping it up and giving it to Janice. It'll bring back memories."

"Excellent idea, Simmons, but you should keep a copy for yourself."

"Okay. I'll take it out and have it copied."

"No! Bring it along. I have a copier."

Qwilleran was curious to see the notebook himself; it might have possibilities.

"Will do, Qwill! See you soon."

"Looking forward to it."

Chiefly Qwilleran was looking forward to having frank discussions with Simmons, on subjects avoided in a small town. Even with his close friends, Polly and Arch, he practiced self-censorship.

Qwilleran drove to Boulder House Inn with a signed copy of *Short & Tall Tales* for Silas Dingwall, who had contributed a hackle-raising legend titled "The Mystery of Dank Hollow." The innkeeper was elated to see his name in print in a book — and his words verbatim. Actually, he was a practiced storyteller, gathering his guests around the craggy fireplace on a cold night and telling ghost stories that had been in his family for generations and rum-running tales that he swore were true.

Qwilleran said to Dingwall, "While I'm here, let's discuss the wedding dinner. All expenses go on my credit card. There'll be three couples, plus one surprise guest from California. Where will you seat us?"

"Ah! We have a glassed-in porch upstairs, for privacy and a view of the lake. And it has an oval table that can be laid with a handsome banquet cloth!"

"Sounds ideal! Let me explain the surprise guest," Qwilleran said.

Dingwall, who enjoyed a little intrigue, said, "We'll hide him in the office until the proper moment. We'll give him a drink — on the house — while he's waiting."

Jovially, Qwilleran said, "I should tell you, Silas, he is the son of a revenue agent."

"I don't care who he's the son of — if he's your friend, he's welcome here!"

"I'd like to order flowers for the table. Any suggestions?"

"Only this. Two low bowls of something instead of one tall arrangement. We use a fine white tablecloth that makes a handsome background for any flowers you choose."

"I'd like Mrs. Duncan to decide on the flowers. May I use your phone?" He called the library and posed the question.

"Lilies!" she said. "Definitely lilies! They're the most extroverted of blossoms, and without the long stems, they have a very appealing personality. And they come in all colors. It would depend greatly on what colors the bride and her attendant are wearing. Do you happen to know?"

"No, I don't happen to know," Qwilleran said, rather testily. More softly he added, "Would you be good enough to call Janice and Sharon MacGillivray and find out?"

"Be glad to," she said. "Then I'll know what to wear."

Qwilleran turned to Dingwall. "It's more complicated than I thought. The florist will deliver the flowers to you Saturday morning."

All the way home from the lakeshore, Qwilleran tried to devise an idea for his Tuesday "Qwill Pen" column. It would have to be original, worthwhile, thought-provoking, entertaining, and easy to write. Nothing came to mind. That meant resorting to another book review.

"Book!" he shouted as he walked into the barn, and Koko soared from the floor to the top shelf and dislodged a slender book that Qwilleran had purchased because it was written by the author of *Alice's Adventures in Wonderland*. Sadly, neither man nor cat had enjoyed it, and it had been relegated to the shelf. Why did the bibliocat draw attention to it again? Koko never did anything without a reason.

Qwilleran packed the tote bag with cats, refreshments, and the paperback copy of *The Hunting of the Snark*. He said, "We all need some fresh air."

They trooped purposefully to the gazebo, and — relaxing in his favorite lounge chair — Qwilleran promptly dozed off. After all, the events of the night had deprived him of sleep.

It was not long before he was aroused by a cacophony of weird sounds from Koko, who was staring through the screen toward the bird garden. There was movement in the shrubbery. Then the branches parted, and out stepped one of those elongated birds with snakelike neck, red wattle, scrawny body, and long, scaly legs.

Then, to compound the mystery, the bird was followed by fifteen or more small replicas, a few inches high. Their composure was definitely greater than that of the watchers in the gazebo. As the cats stared in disbelief, the large bird returned to the shrubbery, followed by the swarm of obedient clones.

On a wild hunch Qwilleran phoned the Hotel Booze and asked Gary, "What's that Turkey Trot announced on the bulletin board in your lobby?"

"That's the monthly meeting of the Outdoor Club. They're having a popular speaker from somewhere in Minnesota. He'll talk about wild turkeys. Everybody welcome. Tomorrow night at seven o'clock. Are you interested in wild turkeys?"

"Just curious."

Chapter Eleven

Qwilleran arrived at the Hotel Booze early for the turkey lecture, hoping to have a burger in a dark corner of the café and then sneak into the meeting hall at the last minute. Unfortunately, his presence at any event led the general public to believe he was covering it for the newspaper or planning to write a "Qwill Pen" column.

An excited crowd could be heard gathering in the lobby, waiting for the doors of the banquet hall to open. More than a hundred seats had been set up. There was plenty of standing room, and Qwilleran slipped in at the last moment, positioning himself near the door — not for fear of fire (although it crossed his mind) but in order to make a swift getaway after the program.

There was an excited hubbub in the hall. Club members had heard tonight's speaker before. There were cries of "Here he comes! Here's Harry!"

An athletic-looking man of middle age jogged down the side aisle of the hall and leaped to the low platform. "Greetings, friends! Any friend of wildlife is a friend of mine."

(Loud response)

The room darkened, and a large screen at the back of the platform filled with a portrait of a long-necked bird with beard, wattles, dewlaps, and saucer eyes.

"This odd-looking creature is the wild turkey. There were flocks of them in the woods when the Pilgrim Fathers landed here, and there are probably millions of them today. Benjamin Franklin suggested making it the national bird, but the old boy had a sense of humor, and I think he was kidding. It would hardly seem appropriate for half the population to be shooting the national bird to put food on the table.

"In many states it is still the chief game bird, with an estimated hundred thousand in some states. Ordinances regulate open seasons, hunting weapons, and even methods of luring the prey. It makes one curious to know more about this remarkable species.

"Most of you (like myself) are nature

lovers and not game hunters, so let me tell you some interesting facts about this unusual species. First of all, did you ever see such a funny-looking geezer? His neck's too long, his head's too small, his eyes are too big, his body is out of proportion! He looks as if he was designed by a committee."

(Laughter)

"But they must have plenty of sex appeal, because they're among the most prolific wildlife. The female lays fifteen eggs. The baby turkeys are called poults."

Qwilleran thought, That's what I saw — a mother turkey with her fifteen poults.

There followed the kind of statistics the audience liked. The wild turkey can run twenty miles an hour and fly fifty miles an hour. The birds roost in the branches of oak and pine trees. They feed on grasses, nuts, berries, and insects. They communicate with clucks, gobbles, yelps, cackles, and purrs.

Qwilleran thought, Ye gods! These are the noises Koko has been making! . . . Where did he learn the language? . . . Has he been luring turkeys back to Moose County after a thirty-year absence? . . . Impossible!

Qwilleran slipped out of the meeting hall. At least it was a comfort to know that the odd-looking creatures in the bird garden were real and not a hallucination.

In the lobby, a pleasant-looking woman was sitting at a long table with stacks of what resembled chocolate brownies in individual plastic sacks.

"Good evening," he said in the musical voice he reserved for such occasions.

"Is the program over?" she asked.

"Not quite. He's showing slides. But I have another appointment."

She saw him staring hungrily at the stack of small bundles on the table. "These are turkey calls," she said. "Harry makes them as a hobby. I'm his wife, Jackie."

He took her extended hand and pressed it warmly. "Your husband is an excellent speaker, and he really knows his subject. You say, Harry makes these?"

"Out of fine hardwood. It's quite an art. It's also therapeutic, too. We lost our two sons in a boating accident at summer camp . . ."

Why, Qwilleran wondered, was she telling him these tragic intimacies? It was, of course, because his sympathetic mien led strangers to unburden themselves.

"Harry channels his emotions into something worthwhile. He sells them at cost to raise money for summer camps for physically challenged children. He donates the total proceeds. There's a wonderful crowd here tonight. I think he'll sell them all."

Jackie was reciting her story so bravely that Qwilleran was moved to say, "How much are they? I'll take three."

"Shall I show you how they work? You don't have to be a hunter, you know, to call turkeys. You can just go out in the woods and hold conversations with the birds, simply by scratching the striker on the hardwood block in different ways."

She demonstrated and gave Qwilleran one to try. It was simple — even primitive. He produced purrs and gobbles and clucks and yelps.

He took the turkey calls home and locked them in a desk drawer and tried not to think about them. He had other things to do. The dress rehearsal was Wednesday night, the Scots were gathering in their tartans on Thursday evening, and he was still collecting material for his column on Agatha Burns. As for Koko, he knew there was something significant in that drawer, and he hung around the desk.

It was unfortunate that Qwilleran had been unable to tape Harry's lecture — the way he described the iridescent plumage of the species, the fanning of the tail with its white stripe, the reddish head of the male and bluish head of the female, and their remarkable field of vision and acute hearing. The ones who visited the barn had apparently heard Koko's clucking and gobbling from the woods where they resided. And since Moose County was said to have no turkeys, they might even have come from the adjoining county!

Then Qwilleran asked himself, Why am I wasting my time on the turkey situation? I have a show to rehearse and a column to write!

On Wednesday at seven p.m., Qwilleran reported to the Hotel Booze with his script, costume, and props, plus a professional-quality recorder and its two satellite speakers, all for the dress rehearsal.

Maxine looked prim in a high-necked shortwaist and a puffy brown wig over her short hair. "It's the Gibson Girl look," she said. "All the rage before World War One. My hairdresser looked it up. The wig just arrived air express."

Qwilleran could not help comparing Maxine's enthusiasm and attention to detail to Lish's cold efficiency and her concern with "What does it pay?"

In the meeting hall, the rows of chairs had been straightened; the platform was equipped with two tables, two chairs, and an old office hall tree on which the newscaster would hang his jacket and hat, after shaking off the fake snow.

"Okay if I watch?" Gary Pratt asked.

Qwilleran stood in the rear hall with door ajar and awaited his cue. The house lights dimmed, the stage lights came up, and Maxine stepped to the front of the stage to deliver her welcoming remarks. Then she sat down at the sound machine, and the WPKX musical signature filled the hall for a minute or two, interrupted by the taped voice of the station announcer reading commercials about fifteen-cent pineapples and motorcars complete with windshields and headlights.

Then, as the music resumed, Qwilleran rushed onstage, throwing off his snow-covered outerwear and glancing anxiously at his watch. Maxine waited for his signal, the music faded, and for the next half hour the newscaster spoke directly to the audience over his fake mike and interviewed eyewitnesses on his fake telephone.

At the end of the rehearsal, Gary rushed to the stage, bellowing, "Bravo!" He clapped the newscaster on the back and hugged the studio engineer. "Come to my office, Qwill, when you've packed your gear. I've got important news for you."

"Good or bad?"

"Both!"

Chapter Twelve

When Qwilleran reported to the hotel office after the dress rehearsal, Gary said, "Your throat must be dry after all that nonstop talking. What'll it be?"

"Squunk water, please. What's the bad news?"

"Lish and Lush are on the way here from Wisconsin!"

"Did she get the letter from the attorney?"

"Apparently, because she wanted to reserve a couple of rooms here. I told her we were sold out for the holiday weekend. She asked if they could park in the lot and sleep in the car. I told her our license doesn't cover campouts. Then she asked for your phone number, Qwill. I thought fast. I told her it had been changed and your number was unlisted."

"You think fast on your feet, Gary."

"Yeah, well . . . I was sitting down. I figured that you didn't want her and her weird boyfriend as houseguests. Anyway, I said she could leave a message for you at the newspaper. You can take it from there. Brrr has plenty of campsites where you can sleep in your car and use the camp facilities, but the thing of it is, I'm afraid she's gonna make a stink about losing Mount Vernon. She's a crafty one! Ask anybody. Do you think I should notify the authorities?"

"It wouldn't hurt!" Qwilleran was beginning to regret he'd commissioned her to research Koko's antecedents. That little four-legged sleuth had known there was something fishy about her from the beginning! "So, what's the good news, Gary?"

"Well! The reservations for the Great Storm show are all taken! We've got to add more performances! Even though there's no charge for admission, they're plunking down ten- and twenty-dollar donations!"

Qwilleran said, "I hope they won't be disappointed. The script isn't as sensational as the one for the Big Burning."

"It's you they want to see and hear, you chump! And what I heard and saw tonight — terrific! We should add Sunday matinees and some more evening performances in July and August."

"Well," he said modestly. Actually, before

switching to journalism, Qwilleran had wanted to act on the stage. (He had also wanted to be a pro ballplayer or jazz pianist, but that was another story.) "How does Maxine feel about added performances? I don't want to make do with substitutes."

"My wife is suddenly stagestruck! She's talking about taking the show on the road!"

Qwilleran spent the next morning polishing his column about Agatha Burns, aware that it should sound like a tribute to a hundred-year-old and not an obituary. There was an early deadline for Friday's *Something*, which would hit the street at ten a.m. with a banner headline: HAPPY 200TH!

He walked downtown to file his copy and stopped at the florist shop to order centerpieces for the wedding dinner. Claudine greeted him effusively, even though her big blue eyes looked at him with apprehension.

"Do you have any short lilies?"

She paused and glanced around the shop. "I never heard of short lilies. They grow on long stems — as a rule, that is. But I could call our supplier in Chicago. How soon do you have to have them?"

"They're for a dinner party Saturday evening, and I've been instructed to order two low arrangements of mixed white and yellow lilies, without any stuffing."

"I suppose we could cut the stems short."

"Do you have low bowls?"

Two low bowls of imitation cut glass were produced and discussed. Was it necessary to have matching bowls? How many blooms would each contain? Four would be too few and six too many, but five would pose a problem: three yellow and two white, or vice versa? The solution: one bowl with white predominating and the other with yellow predominating, to be delivered to the Boulder House for the Qwilleran table.

Showing much relief, Claudine said she would phone Chicago at once.

In the early afternoon, Qwilleran wandered into the classiest shop in town.

Modest gold lettering in one corner of the plate-glass window stated: EXBRIDGE & COBB, FINE ANTIQUES.

Qwilleran asked Susan Exbridge, "Do you ever have any miniature porcelain shoes?"

"No, but I know where to find some. Are you starting a collection? There are some serious collectors here and in Lockmaster."

"I've just met one of them, Edythe Carroll. She invited me to tea the other day, and I thought I'd like to send her a shoe."

"I wouldn't advise it," Susan said. "Her collection is a very private matter, pursued by her and her husband throughout their married life. She has told me she wants no more, now that he's gone. The last shoe they found together was a Meissen porcelain while they were vacationing in Germany. Edythe keeps it on her bedside table."

Qwilleran nodded sympathetically. "I quite understand. There must be a hundred or more in her glass-front cabinet. I must say that miniature shoes strike me as a strange item to collect. What's the story behind them?"

"Come in the office for a cup of coffee and I'll tell you what I know."

Every inch of wall space in the office was covered with shelves — for reference books on antiques. Susan noted his appreciative glance at them. "These books belonged to dear Iris Cobb. I owe so much to her."

"We all do," Qwilleran said, as he sipped his coffee. Then — "On the question about the shoes, why were they made in the first place?"

"In Victorian times they held matches, toothpicks, salt, snuff. Some were pincushions. There was a great demand for them in the nineteenth century, and porcelain factories in many European countries were turning out high-heeled shoes, boots, slippers, and oxfords — with all kinds of decorations: flowers, birds, cherubs, and so forth. Collectors make a study of the dates, makers' marks, glazes, et cetera. Prices can run as high as a thousand."

"Hmmm," Qwilleran murmured into his moustache. "You know a great deal about the subject, considering you don't handle it in your shop."

"I've been spending long hours with Edythe," Susan explained. "After her husband died, she asked me to help her update the catalogue of her antiques in Mount Vernon. Most were handed down in her family. She was a Goodwinter, you know. And now that she's decided to donate the house and contents to the community, as a museum, it's important to have accurate descriptions and values. When she moved to Ittibittiwassee, I helped her select the pieces she wanted to keep. Most important was the china cabinet filled with shoes. Why am I telling you all this?"

"Because you know I'm interested and concerned."

"And you're not a gossip. Darling!" She returned to the brittle style she affected. "Are you sure you don't want to buy something before you leave?"

"How much do you want for that ten-foot breakfront?"

"You couldn't afford it!" She chased him out of the store.

For Scottish night, Qwilleran wore a kilt in the Mackintosh tartan — red with a fine green line. Polly wore a tartan sash looped under one arm and pinned on the opposite shoulder with a cairngorm; the Duncans shared a colorful tartan with the Robertson clan.

"Qwill! You look so wonderful. I think I shall cry!" she said.

"It's a matter of the swagger that comes with a kilt. The devil-may-care tilt of a glengarry bonnet over the right eye, the toughness of knowing there's a dagger in the cuff of one's knee hose, and the pride of being a Mackintosh."

"I've noticed that persons not entitled to wear Scottish attire seem very . . . ordinary by comparison," Polly observed with a note of pity in her voice.

The ordinary ones stayed home Thursday night and watched the festivities on television. The TV crews had been in town all day.

In the early evening, the streets radiating

from the Hotel Booze were filled with canny Scots who had parked on the outskirts and were walking toward the hub of activity. It was a kaleidoscope of clan tartans in vibrant reds, greens, blues, yellows, and combinations thereof. The wearers all had the quiet pride that Qwilleran had mentioned. He and Polly stopped to have a few words with the MacGillivrays, then the Campbells, the Ogilvies, the MacLeods, and more Campbells.

A hush fell on the crowd when the bell in the tower of the town hall tolled seven times. All eyes turned toward the hotel, and out came Chief Andrew Brodie with the lofty feather bonnet of a bagpiper, swaggering with a shoulder full of plaid and an armful of pipes. He was playing "Scotland the Brave." Following him was Mayor Ramsey, pushing a wheelchair. The occupant was the centenarian, Miss Agatha Burns — fragile, calm, smiling. How many hearts turned over at the sight of her. Even those who had not been in one of her classes knew about the Burns mystique.

Arriving at a low platform near the bandstand and the birthday cake, the mayor accepted a microphone and declared that the historic town of Brrr had reached its two-hundredth year. Miss Agatha pressed a button, and the two hundred electric candles on the wooden cake were dazzling in the approaching dusk.

After that there were refreshments in the hotel and some serious marmalade tasting . . . entertainment in the park . . . conversation among Scots . . . Lisa and Lyle Compton were there. (She was a Campbell — her husband a Ross.) Polly said they looked splendid in tartans. Lyle applauded the "Qwill Pen" column on Miss Agatha Burns. Qwilleran asked, "Lyle, are you both attending the dedication of the Carroll Memorial Museum Sunday afternoon?" He said they wouldn't miss it for anything! Lisa said that Edythe would turn over the keys to Mount Vernon, and someone would give her an armful of roses. Then they discussed the Marmalade Madness and the merits of each. Polly said the bookstore was getting a marmalade mascot named Dundee.

When Qwilleran drove Polly back to Indian Village, he declined her invitation to come in for some music. Polly said with a sigh, "I should really bear down on my studying. I'm learning some amazing facts. Do you realize that a bookstore grossing fifty thousand dollars will need one-point-eight persons on the staff?"

"Where do you get eight-tenths of a person?" Qwilleran said. "I feel that way myself sometimes, but I wouldn't admit it to a prospective employer."

Polly, who had become an expert at ignoring his levity, went on: "What do you think about having the cashier and service counter on the left as one enters? They say traffic flows in normally to the right and continues out on the other side."

"Will Dundee have a location of his own? Or will he be free to wander at will?"

"That topic hasn't been covered in my manual," Polly said. "Mac and Katie at the library have simply adopted the circulation desk as their headquarters."

After taking Polly home, Qwilleran drove back to Pickax faster than usual, as if a strange force was pulling him back to the barn. He had felt it before, when the cats had needed him.

The answer was waiting for him in the barnyard: a station wagon with a Wisconsin tag. But there were no cats waiting in the window. They were in hiding. The trespassers were probably in the gazebo.

Qwilleran grabbed a high-powered flashlight from his car and walked stealthily around to the front of the barn before switching it on.

Shocked and blinded by the sudden light, Lish and Lush jumped to their feet.

"Aren't you people at the wrong address?" Qwilleran thundered. They had been drinking beer and eating take-out food.

"I'm sorry, Mr. Qwilleran. I couldn't find a phone number for you. This is Clarence, my driver. I can't have a license. Health problem, you know."

Clarence gave a dopey nod, and Qwilleran responded accordingly.

Lish went on with characteristic nerve. "Do you happen to have a guest room we could use? All the accommodations are booked solid."

Qwilleran said, "I have only one guest room, and that is occupied by a friend from California — a police investigator, here to work on a case." He saw an involuntary glance pass between the two. "However, there are plenty of campsites where you can sleep in your car and use camp facilities. The best is Great Oaks. I'll tell you how to get there. Have you brought a report on the matter I discussed with you?"

160

"No, but I have notes and can tell you the whole story."

"Then excuse me a moment while I feed the cats."

The Siamese had been fed earlier, but it was a chance to pick up his pocket tape recorder and a checkbook.

Back in the gazebo he said, "Okay, sit down and let's hear it."

"It ended up taking a lot more time than I expected, but I was on the trail of something important, so I persevered.

"First I checked the phone book, as you suggested, and there was no Mountclemens or Bonifield listed. So I thought of going to the courthouse. There were records in several different departments that might give a clue, and I spent a couple of days there. Then I had some vital business to take care of, so I turned the search over to one of the clerks. She was very nice, and eager to help. I told her to keep a record of hours spent and she'd be reimbursed.

"Well, it paid off! When I went back, she was all excited, saying it made her feel like a detective. There was no Mountclemens, but there was a Monty Clemens, who was the son of a George Clemens, and his mother had been Bonnie Field before her marriage. Monty was an artist who became an art critic somewhere out of town. He could have changed his name to George Bonifield Mountclemens, to sound more important than Monty Clemens.

"George was dead, but Bonnie was living in a nursing home in the suburbs, and I found her there. When she said she'd been a cat breeder, I felt as if we'd struck gold! She raised Persians.

"Well, George went to Southeast Asia during the Vietnam War, and when it was over, he got a traveling job doing business in Bangkok. He went back and forth several times a year and told his wife about the gorgeous cats they had there. What's more, they kept records of their heritage, tracing some of them back to the days when Thailand was called Siam, and the cats were bred as watch cats in the royal courts. They were known to be highly intelligent, and some had traits that were positively supernatural! The super cats weren't usually sold to foreigners, but George knew the right people and had done favors for people, so they agreed to sell him a pedigreed male.

"When he phoned Bonnie, she was thrilled and told him she needed a breeding pair. So he pulled some more strings and got a female. They were very expensive, she said. Next problem: how to get them into the U.S. without the quarantine. George pulled some more strings, and the pair crossed the Pacific on an Air Force jet, probably howling all the way, Bonnie said with a laugh.

"So your cat is descended from this original breeding pair. Bonnie stopped breeding Persians and concentrated on Siamese. She did very well. All her customers reported that their cats had ESP."

"Very interesting, Lish," Qwilleran said. "How much do I owe you?"

"Well, it was a lot of fun, and I'd love to do it for nothing, Mr. Qwilleran, but there were a lot of expenses: travel cost and remuneration to the courthouse clerk and Bonnie Field. I thought you'd want me to be generous. The clerk spent a lot of hours, and Bonnie really needed the money. She said there are no retirement benefits for cat breeders. And I spent a total of nineteen hours myself, including travel time. So I think a thousand would be fair, less the fifty that you gave me in advance."

"I'll write you a check."

"Could you possibly make it cash? It's hard to get a large check cashed when you're on the road, the way I am."

"I . . . well . . . how would it be if I make the check payable to cash, and I'll tell Gary

Pratt at the Hotel Booze to cash it for you. Hotels always have money in the safe."

Qwilleran clicked off the recorder surreptitiously, thanked Lish for her conscientious work, wrote her a check, and stood up briskly, signifying: end of interview.

She kicked her driver's ankle (he had dozed off) and said she would be happy to undertake other assignments in the future.

"Where can I reach you in Milwaukee?" Qwilleran asked.

"Well, I'm in the process of relocating, and I'm not sure where. I'll get back to you."

"Do that!" he said. "Now, I'll give you directions for reaching the Great Oaks camp."

He watched their taillights receding through the woods before going indoors to brew a cup of coffee and contemplate the whole fabricated farce.

Chapter Thirteen

 Following the welcome departure of Lish and Lush, Qwilleran observed the cats' bedtime ritual and then settled down with a mug of coffee to consider . . .

- That he could have invented a better story himself, based on documented history;
- That Lish kept moistening her lips all the time she was relating "discoveries";
- That she had been careful not to give her address;
- That she and Lush had exchanged startled glances when a police investigator was mentioned;
- Then, perhaps more important, how Koko reacted with bared fangs and subtle snarl whenever there was any reference to Alicia Carroll.

As for the thousand-dollar scam, it could be written off as a legitimate expense in the book Qwilleran hoped to write: *The Private Life of the Cat Who . . .*

The Fourth of July was like any other date on the calendar to the pampered Siamese who reported for breakfast. To Qwilleran it meant the opening night of the "Great Storm" show.

First he phoned Gary Pratt and authorized the cashing of the check.

"Wow! Is that what she charged you?" the hotelier asked in surprise. "Was it worth it? Did you learn anything?"

"I learned quite a few things" was the ambiguous answer. "Now I'm concentrating on opening night. How's Maxine?"

"She's always up-up-up. Is there anything we can do for you?"

"Well, I don't like to eat a full meal before a performance, but I'd like a hearty breakfast, so . . . what better venue than the Black Bear Café? I want to mosey around Brrr and eavesdrop on the tourists . . . and see the beginning of the boat parade . . . and watch the kids making wishes and blowing out electric candles . . . and then home for a nap before curtain time."

The modest town of Brrr was again ablaze with excitement. Gone were the Scottish tartans! In their place were posters and T-shirts flaunting the "Brrr 200" symbol in red, white, and blue. Pushcarts were offering the shirts in five sizes, and tourists were stripping off their shirts and substituting the bicentennial badge right there on the sidewalk.

In the park across from the hotel, the entertainment was continuous, and youngsters and adults alike lined up to make a birthday wish and blow out the electric candles.

Along the shore there was a manic anticipation of the boat parade, as two hundred cabin cruisers — in eight harbors — awaited their signal. At noon the first fleets would leave Fishport on the west and Deep Harbor on the east. Spectators with cameras and binoculars crowded every vantage point, including housetops along the shoreline.

At noon, when the town hall bell tolled twelve, silence fell in downtown Brrr until an announcement came over loudspeakers that the first fleet had just left Fishport. A shout was raised! After fifteen minutes it was announced that the Mooseville fleet had joined the parade, and the Brrr contingent should be ready to go in eight minutes.

All eyes strained toward the western horizon. When the first craft loomed into view, spectators screamed and jumped for joy! Within minutes, boats flying American flags sailed past the harbor of Brrr, cabin cruisers with three-foot flags.

It was an emotional moment for the watchers on shore. Some happy tears were shed. There was an awed stillness. The second fleet followed, from Mooseville; and then the Brrr contingent sailed off.

Qwilleran shook his head as he thought of "The Great Storm of 1913." The parade of boats would be a hard act to follow.

Qwilleran arrived at the Hotel Booze an hour before curtain time.

Gary said, "Anything I can do you for? Anything you want to eat or drink?"

"All I need is a quiet place to get into my role."

Together they checked the back hall from which the newscaster would make his "entrance." All it offered were two rest rooms, a broom closet, and a storage room for hotel furniture. It was a jumble of chairs and tables, with a little floor space for pacing. Qwilleran moved in.

At one point Maxine dropped in and asked him to listen to her opening speech.

He listened and suggested a significant pause of two seconds in the middle of the last sentence. "You'll capture their attention, arouse their curiosity, and enlist their cooperation. Try it."

She tried! "We are going to ask you to imagine . . . that home radios really existed in 1913 . . . as we bring you a broadcast covering the Great Storm of that year."

As curtain time approached, Qwilleran opened the door to the stage — just enough to hear the babbling audience, the sudden hush when the house lights dimmed, the murmur that greeted the appearance of the Gibson Girl shirtwaist and wig, the rustling of programs as she began to speak, and then the dead silence when she said, "We are going to ask you to imagine —"

As she sat down at the controls, a burst of music came from the two speakers, followed by a few commercials that produced tittering in the audience. Again, more music, during which Qwilleran made his entrance and shook the fake snow from his clothing. Then the newscaster spoke in his compelling stage voice:

The late evening news is a little late tonight, folks. Blame it on the weather: snow,

snow, and more snow. First, a look at the headlines . . .

(Reading) Sunday, November ninth. A violent storm with heavy snow and high winds has been blasting Moose County and the lake, with no relief in sight. Elsewhere in the nation . . .

In Washington, President Woodrow Wilson is predicting war with Mexico.

In New York, visitors at an art show were so infuriated by the paintings on exhibition that they rioted in the street; two policemen were injured.

Meanwhile, here at home, blizzard conditions have paralyzed Moose County. Visibility is zero, as a heavy snowfall is whipped by fifty-mile-an-hour winds. Drifting snow is making roads impassable. In downtown Pickax, not a wagon or pedestrian can be seen. Even sleighs cannot get through; horses can make no headway against the wind.

The storm has taken this area by surprise. Following the recent turbulence on the lake, weather conditions settled down to normal yesterday, and shipping was resumed. A steady traffic in freighters and passenger boats could be seen moving north for the last run of the season. Even though the Weather Bureau predicted more disturbances in the atmosphere, the sun was shining and the temperature was unusually high for November. Today, in the early-morning hours, there was still no weather to discourage duck hunters from going out on the Bay. This being Sunday, the commercial fishermen were taking a day off, and a peaceful calm descended on the shoreline. It was the lull before the storm.

Shortly after daybreak, the wind began to rise, and the sky turned the color of copper — a most unusual sight, according to early risers. By ten a.m., winds of fifty miles an hour were recorded. Churchgoers returning home on foot or even in buggies found the going difficult. One small boy was torn away from his mother's hand by a sudden gust, and he rolled down Main Street like a tumbleweed.

Snow started to fall in the afternoon. It has accumulated steadily. Eight inches was first predicted. Now twelve or even eighteen inches is not unlikely. Drifting snow on country roads and city streets is piling up — six feet deep in some locations. And this may be only the beginning, according to weather experts.

Here is a bulletin from Fishport: Two duck hunters from Down Below left shore early this morning — two miles south of town. They have not been seen since that time. Their boat has been found, bottom-up, on the shore.

According to a bulletin from Deep Harbor, a passenger boat from Down Below was unable to reach port here because of damage to her stern rudder. She was last seen steaming backward down the lake.

No bulletins have been received from the Lifesaving Station, but we hope to reach them for a firsthand report on conditions at Purple Point.

(Picks up phone) Operator, this is WPKX calling Brrr Harbor Lifesaving Station. . . . Yes, we know. But please do the best you can. . . . Thank you. . . . Brrr Harbor Station? Is it possible to speak to the captain? WPKX calling. . . . Captain, this is the radio newsroom in Pickax. What is the storm situation up there?

CAPTAIN ON TAPE: Bad! Very bad! Worst I've ever seen. There's a vessel stranded on the reef here. She's being battered by the waves. We can't reach her. Made two tries. Wrecked both of our rescue boats. Lucky to get our crew back alive. We tried our small boat, too. Put it on a sledge and had the horses pull it down the beach, closer to the wreck. No good. Boat got as far as Seagull Island and filled with water. Had to turn back. We've still got the surfboat, but it's buried in frozen sand.

NEWSCASTER: Captain, what is the name of the vessel on the reef?

CAPTAIN ON TAPE: Can't tell. Must be a freighter. They're blowing a distress signal, but it's hard to hear. Wind is shrieking. Waves are roaring and booming like cannon. Can't see anything. Can't see two feet in front of your face. Snow comes at you like a white blanket.

NEWSCASTER: Sir, is there any chance of saving the crew of the freighter? How many are aboard, would you estimate?

CAPTAIN ON TAPE: Probably twenty-five or more. If she's battered to pieces by morning, the whole crew could be lost. In this icy water, a man wouldn't last twenty minutes. There are signs of life out there *now*, we think, but the cabin's washed away and she must be flooded below-decks. Whole vessel will be a block of ice by morning.

NEWSCASTER: Yesterday was a beautiful

day, Captain. Where did this storm come from?

CAPTAIN ON TAPE: Can't say. Seems to be coming from two directions. Never saw anything like it. Wind is sixty-two knots — more than seventy miles an hour. That's gale force! Temperature below freezing. Whole shore covered with ice. Our wharfs and boathouse are beginning to break up. My men are taking it hard. They want to go after those poor devils out there, but there's nothing they can do. We're helpless.

NEWSCASTER: Thank you, Captain. We'll hope and pray for the best.

Here are more bulletins from towns around the shoreline.

From Mooseville: Six duck hunters rented a launch early this morning and headed for Lone Tree Island. The owner of the launch is positive it could not withstand this heavy sea. The persistent north wind has raised the water level in the bay, and if the hunters are marooned on Lone Tree, there is little hope. The island could be submerged by this time.

From Port George: Wharfs and sheds belonging to the commercial fisheries are being shattered by mountainous waves. Even buildings set back from the shore are losing doors, windows, and chimneys. One section of the beach is littered with a jumble of freshly cut timber. Rafts of logs, being floated to the sawmill, have broken loose and are being tossed on the shore like matchsticks.

Here's one from Purple Point: The community pier has been demolished, along with cargo awaiting shipment: a thousand barrels of apples and twenty-five tons of baled hay.

Serious news from Trawnto Beach: The lightship that warns vessels away from the shoals has been torn from its moorings, increasing the danger to freighters that have lost their course in the blinding snowstorm. Large steel freighters are being tossed by winds up to eighty miles an hour. Boats trying to turn and head back are rolling wildly in the trough of thirty-five-foot waves. The Lifesaving Station has been completely destroyed.

(Consults watch) Our Deep Harbor correspondent is standing by. (Picks up phone) Operator, this is WPKX. Can you connect us with the mobile unit in Deep Harbor?

TAPE OF HIGH WIND AND WAVES, THEN
    VOICE-OVER: Here in Deep Harbor the noise is deafening: the howling of

the wind, the crashing of huge waves, the cracking and groaning of wooden structures breaking up. A wave hits the concrete breakwater, and it sounds like an explosion. The *old* breakwater, built of wood, is reduced to splinters. The noise drowns out the distress signals from the big boats. They're frantic for help, but the lifesaving boats have been smashed on the rocks.

The lake is reaching farther inland than anyone can remember. The fisheries have lost buildings, boats, piers, and nets. Houses near the shore are being lifted from their foundations. There'll be no sleep for anyone on the shore tonight. Over. Back to Pickax.

NEWSCASTER: Hang on, Deep Harbor. While residents of shore communities are ready to evacuate their homes at a moment's notice, families living inland are advised to stay indoors. One farmer attempting to open his barn door was buried alive in an avalanche when the wind whipped in and filled the barn with snow in a matter of seconds.

The entire county is now isolated. Telegraph lines are down. Railway trains are at a standstill. Passenger trains from Down Below have been halted by drifts, and travelers are stranded. The destruction of boats and docks means that Moose County's major lifeline has been cut. Food, coal, and kerosene will not reach this area for many days.

In Pickax, all establishments are closed and will remain closed until further notice. Even emergency services have found it impossible to respond to calls. Firefighters, doctors, and police report they are blinded and completely disoriented by the whirlwind of snow.

When the storm is over, volunteers will be needed immediately to assist road crews in digging out the city.

Meanwhile, city officials issue this warning: Stay indoors, and conserve food and fuel. Repeat: Stay indoors, and conserve food and fuel. And please stay tuned to WPKX for further directives.

This is WPKX signing off for Sunday, November ninth.

Qwilleran made his exit as the stage lights dimmed and storm music of *Francesca da Rimini* filled the hall. Moments later he returned, wearing other garb and carrying another script. His manner was somber as he signaled to Maxine. The music faded away, and the stage lights came up:

Wednesday, November twelfth. The worst storm in the history of the lake is now just a tragic memory, as Moose County tries to assess the damage and pick up the pieces. Farmers report livestock frozen in the fields. Commercial fisheries have lost their means of livelihood. Since fishing is a major industry on the North Shore, the economic impact on Moose County could be serious. The entire shore-line is littered with wreckage: wharfs, commercial buildings, fishing boats, houses, pleasure craft, summer cottages, and government rescue stations. Worst of all is the loss of life. Almost two hundred sailors were drowned, and bodies are still washing up on the Canadian shore. In rural areas, many persons are reported missing. It is now presumed that they lost their way in the blizzard and have frozen to death.

A Lifesaving Station was able to rescue the crew of the five-hundred-foot steamer *Hanna*, wrecked on the reef. They were rescued after thirty-six hours of desperate attempts. Twenty-five officers and men — and a woman cook who was praised for her bravery — were brought safely to shore by the surfboat. The wreckage will remain on the reef until spring, when salvage operations will begin.

Many crews were less fortunate. Boats capsized or broke in two or "crumpled like eggshells," according to one observer. What appeared to be a large whale, drifting in the lake, was the hull of a large freighter, upside down and kept afloat by air bubbles. It later sank to the bottom.

Among the fortunate survivors of the storm were six duck hunters who went out before the storm and were marooned all night on Lone Tree Island. They were rescued on Monday, suffering from exposure and on the verge of pneumonia. One of them is standing by to give our listeners a firsthand account of a terrifying adventure.

(Picks up phone) Operator, ready for the Mooseville call. Hello. Yes, this is the WPKX newsroom. Sir, will you tell us how you happened to be out on that island during the storm?

HUNTER ON TAPE: Well, me and five other fellas rented a boat Sunday mornin' and went out to the island for some birds. We was just gettin' set up when the wind come up. Nobody thought much about it. But then I heard that spooky whistlin' sound that means trouble. We was two miles from the mainland, and I wanted to get the heck out of there. But the other fellas, they wanted to get a few shots before quittin'. The wind got real bad then. Even the ducks, they was flyin' backwards, like.

We could see our boat tossin' around, and the first thing we know, she broke loose and headed for open water. By that time it was gettin' awful cold. There we was — alone on an island with nothin' but a little shack and some miserable trees. We was dressed warm, but we went to the shack and made a fire in the little stove there. Next thing, it started to snow. I never seen such a blizzard. All around us — nothin' but white. And then the lake, she started to rise. Kept creepin' closer to the shack. We huddled around the stove until the water busted right in and put the fire out. Whole island was flooded. By the time it got dark, we was standin' in freezin' water up to our waist. Somebody said we should tie ourselves together with a piece o' rope. Don't know why, but we did. Then the shanty, it started to move. We're gonna be swept into the bay, I thought. But that durned shanty got stuck between a coupla trees, and there we hung, like trapped animals.

NEWSCASTER: Sir, how long did the blow continue?

HUNTER ON TAPE: Musta been sixteen, eighteen hours. Calmed down about two in the mornin', and we was still there, shiverin' and tied together, when they come lookin' for us, in a boat from Mooseville.

NEWSCASTER: What did you do to keep your spirits up during this . . . this nightmare? I mean, did you talk? Sing? Tell jokes?

HUNTER ON TAPE: (Pause) Well, we talked — we talked about our families. And I guess we prayed a lot.

NEWSCASTER: Thank you, sir. We're glad you all got back alive. And take care of that cough!

The news from Fishport was not so good. The bodies of two duck hunters were washed up on the beach, not far from the spot where their wrecked boat was found.

Near Deep Harbor, the storm tossed up a gruesome reminder of an unsolved mystery. Seven years ago, a tugboat with a crew of five disappeared just outside the harbor.

According to eyewitnesses, one minute it was there, and the next minute it was gone. No trace of boat or crew was ever found. During Sunday's storm, the waves churned up the smokestack and cabin of this long-lost boat. With it was one body, badly decomposed after seven summers and seven winters at the bottom of the lake. Deep Harbor also reports that the concrete breakwater failed to withstand the pounding of the waves. Three hundred feet of the breakwater washed away, the waves rolling huge chunks of concrete like marbles.

The storm has raised many puzzling questions. How can one explain the abnormal behavior of wind and water? According to the United States Weather Bureau, it was a clash of *three* low-pressure fronts — one coming down from Alaska, one from the Rocky Mountains, and a third from the Gulf of Mexico. They met over the lake.

A spokesman for the Weather Bureau has stated that gale warnings were flown at all stations. The signal flags are well known to sailors — the red square with a black center, flown over a white pennant. *But the skippers of the big freighters ignored the warnings. Why?*

A retired lake captain, who wishes to remain anonymous, gave WPKX his explanation.

SCOTTISH CAPTAIN ON TAPE: Greed, that's what it's all about. Greed! The owners of the boats put pressure on the skippers to squeeze in one or two more voyages at the end of the season. It means more profit for the company and maybe a promotion for the skipper and a bonus for the crew, so they don't heed the storm warnings. Many a lake captain has taken the gamble. But this storm was a fierce one. It was a gamble that no man could win.

NEWSCASTER: The result of last Sunday's gamble: eight freighters sunk . . . 188 lives lost . . . nine other large boats wrecked or grounded . . . millions of dollars lost in vessels and cargo. But no one can estimate the cost of the terror and heartache caused by the Great Storm of 1913. And no one who has lived through this storm will ever forget it.

Chapter Fourteen

 "Millions of dollars lost . . . But no one can estimate the cost of the terror and heartache caused by the Great Storm of 1913. And no one who has lived through this storm will ever forget it." The newscaster spoke the words with deep feeling and threw down his script in a final gesture of regret and sorrow. The stage blacked out.

Immediately the audience erupted in applause and cheers, rising to their feet en masse.

The lights came up and Qwilleran stood and bowed and extended an arm toward his assistant, who rose and bowed. There were more shouts. She looked at Qwilleran for a cue, and they both made an exit through the door at stage rear. Maxine said, "Applause is kind of intoxicating, isn't it? I think they were applauding my wig."

"They were applauding your presence,"

Qwilleran assured her, "and your gracious introduction."

"I'd never been on a stage before an audience. I was too shy to be in school plays or even Sunday school pageants."

Her husband appeared from nowhere. "Sweetie! You were wonderful! Qwill! Your performance was hypnotic! And the script was powerful!"

"It was the real thing, that's all," Qwilleran said modestly. "Everyone in the audience has family members who were there!"

"Yeah, my grandparents lived through it. They always brought up the subject at family reunions. Well, how about coming into the bar to celebrate, Qwill?"

"Thanks, but I'll celebrate at the end of the run. I've got a big day tomorrow. I've got to go home and shift gears."

"And feed the cats," said Gary, who had heard it before.

Driving home, Qwilleran assessed the audience response. In Moose County, a live program of any kind was a special event; good or bad, it called for enthusiastic hand clapping and screams. As for standing ovations, the audience, he believed, was simply getting ready to go home. At tonight's performance, they applauded the magnitude of his moustache as much as his dramatic skills. He knew he was a good writer, and he was a good reader of lines. He had spent all those hours reading aloud to the cats.

As he drove into the barnyard, his headlights illuminated the rear of the building, and there in the kitchen window was Koko, giving him a standing ovation!

The male cat was always a bundle of nervous energy, reporting that there was a message on the answering machine, or a meal was past due, or there had been a stranger on the premises. Yum Yum always hung back and looked worried.

On this occasion, Koko had pushed a volume off the shelf. It was *The Hunting of the Snark* — not one of Qwilleran's favorites: He substituted the poems of Robert Service and indulged himself in the macho rhythms of the Yukon. *A bunch of the boys were whooping it up in the Malamute saloon.*

Simmons arrived on the Saturday-morning shuttle flight. Qwilleran picked him up at the airport.

"Janice is a nice woman," the visitor said. "Glad to see that she's finally getting married. Who is the guy?"

"John Bushland, prizewinning photographer and one of my best friends. He likes to be called Bushy and makes a joke of the fact that he's losing his hair."

"I hope he likes waffles. And parrots. Where's the dinner being held?"

"At the Boulder House Inn, a picturesque place on the shore. You and I will arrive early, and the innkeeper will hide you in his office with a drink. The rest of us meet on the parapet overlooking the lake. Just as we are about to toast the newlyweds, you enter. . . ."

"And the bride has a heart attack," Simmons guessed.

They had arrived at the barn, where Simmons had been a guest on his previous visit. "It doesn't look a day older," he remarked of the century-old barn.

He was greeted by the Siamese, who treated him like an old friend. "They're very handsome creatures. The big one looks frighteningly intelligent, if you ask me, and the little one is a flirt."

They were sitting in the lounge area, having coffee and Scotch shortbread.

"You know, Qwill," he went on, "I never really paid any close attention to cats, but my mother — Lottie was her name — was crazy about them. After she died, I started seeing cats through her eyes! I'd look at a strange cat and know exactly what Lottie would say. It kind of shook me up."

"Consider it your inheritance from Lottie," Qwilleran said. "My mother died when I was in college, majoring in baseball and jazz bands. Suddenly I became interested in *words!* I switched to journalism, started writing a book, joined the Shakespeare Club. There's only one way I can explain it: She had bequeathed me her love of words. She was a librarian."

At five o'clock that evening, Simmons was undercover at the Boulder House, while Qwilleran and Polly were on the parapet with the newly wedded couple and their attendants. Bushy, Roger, and Qwilleran were bonded in friendship, having been shipwrecked on an island during a violent summer storm.

The three couples looked festive but informal: Janice, Sharon, and Polly in short-sleeved pastel dresses; the three men in white summer jackets, summer shirts, and no ties.

The men were talking about their ordeal. At that moment, they were joined by another man in a light-blue summer jacket.

Janice screamed, "Simmons! What are you doing here?"

"Just looking for a drink," he said.

Concealed under his coat was a worn school notebook, which he handed to the bride. *"Secrets of Thelma's Dinner Club."*

Janice was overcome. She said, "I'd faint if I wasn't having such a good time!"

When the newlyweds were asked about their plans, they said that they would live in Thelma's wonderful house on Pleasant Street; Bushy would no longer rent space for a commercial studio; a darkroom could be installed in the basement; Janice was learning the fine points of developing and printing; portrait photography could be done in the handsome main rooms of the house.

Then they extended an invitation to everyone for the next day: a cruise among the picturesque offshore islands, with a picnic lunch aboard while anchored near the lighthouse. Bushy had a great cabin cruiser named the *View Finder*, and Janice was noted for her exciting picnic lunches. And they would see that Simmons got to the airport in time for the five-o'clock shuttle.

Simmons accepted the invitation with pleasure. So did the MacGillivrays. So did Polly.

Only Qwilleran had to decline, saying that he was doing a matinee at two o'clock.

Then the storytelling began: Simmons, about Thelma's dinner club; Janice, about Thelma's parrots; Polly, about embarrassing questions that librarians are asked.

Dinner was served in the glassed-in porch. The oval table was laid with a white banquet cloth and centered with two bowls of lilies in mixed white and yellow. They talked with exuberance, reminisced endlessly, laughed a lot, and had a good time. If anyone noticed it, the food was excellent. And the serving of dessert coincided with the setting of the sun over a hundred miles of lake.

The party ended with hugs, handshakes, and felicitations. The Bushlands and the MacGillivrays took home the bowls of white and yellow lilies. Qwilleran dropped off Polly at Indian Village and drove to the barn with his houseguest.

Simmons said, "Very interesting woman, Polly. You don't often hear such a pleasant voice. Has she ever been married? What's the bookstore she mentioned?"

"It's being built in downtown Pickax, where the previous bookstore stood for fifty years before being torched."

"Did they get the arsonist?"

"He and two coconspirators are in prison. The old building was built in 1850 by a blacksmith who moonlighted as a pirate, and his loot was said to be buried under what had become a parking lot. At the official groundbreaking for the new store, thousands of people came from all over the county to see the pirate's gold coins. The chest was found, but it was empty."

"How did the crowd react. Did they riot?"

"They thought it was a good joke! This is Moose County, not Los Angeles."

When they arrived at the barn, Qwilleran said, "Would you like a nightcap? Or a refresher?"

"I'd like to try that Squunk water you drink."

"Red or white?"

"Oh. Red."

They sat around the big square cocktail table, and Qwilleran gave him a book. "Take this home. It's a collection of legends that has just been published — all about pirates, ghosts, and other wholesome subjects. You can read it to your grandchildren. Do you read to them?"

"Yes, but the eight-year-old reads to me! Do you still read to your cats?"

"I do, and if Koko starts *reading to me*, I'm really going to get worried."

Simmons asked, "What's that book on the floor?"

"Koko keeps pushing it off the shelf, expecting me to read it aloud. It's *The Hunting of the Snark*."

"What's a snark? Sounds like something spelled backwards."

"It's a cross between a snake and a shark — just nonsense verses. Koko seems to sense it's by the author of *Alice's Adventures in Wonderland*, which is one of his favorites."

Koko knew he was being talked about, and he made his presence known.

Simmons said, "Friendly cuss, isn't he?"

"He knows you're a cop. He likes cops."

"Which reminds me," Simmons said, "on the phone you mentioned an incident that happened on your property. What was that all about?"

"I have a hundred acres of beach frontage, and a well-dressed male was killed execution-style in a wooded area there. No ID or valuables on the body. The SBI is handling the case. Meanwhile, our police chief tells me there's been a similar incident in northern Michigan."

Simmons nodded. "I remember an identical case out west. A guy hung around a sportsmen's bar, talking about hunting and fishing and saying he knew a great spot for a hunting lodge. He showed snapshots of a lake with ducks flying and a trout stream with a waterfall. The property belonged to a friend who had to sell it to pay a child-support judgment or go to prison. He would sell it for a tenth of its value. He found a sucker who drove up into the hills with him and his friend, both crooks. They had a fake surveyor's map and a fake title — and a gun. The sucker had the cash. And that was the end of him and his great deal!"

"Did they ever solve the case?"

"Not until it happened in a nearby state, and the investigators were able to trace a pattern. That's the pity of it; there's always some sucker looking for a fantastic deal."

Qwilleran said, "I hear that land fraud goes on all the time without the homicide — because people are ignorant or greedy."

Koko looked up briefly from his empty plate and said, "Yow!"

"Why is he staring at me?" Simmons asked.

"Look at your watch."

"It's eleven o'clock."

"He wants his bedtime snack. Would you like to feed him?"

"Me? How do I do it?"

"See that glass jar on the kitchen counter?

It's full of homemade crunchies. Just put half a cupful on one plate and a little less on the other. Then put them on the floor under the kitchen table. Koko's goes on the right."

Simmons followed instructions, at the same time saying, "Look, Ma! I'm feeding a cat."

For the Sunday matinee there was another full house at the Hotel Booze, and a greater air of excitement prevailed; show-goers had heard from friends and relatives how the imaginary broadcast was a retelling of family history. During the performance an occasional whimpering in the audience came, perhaps from the granddaughter of the farmer who had been buried under an avalanche of snow in his own barn, or a descendant of a lifesaving crewman who had participated in a heroic rescue. When it was over, the listeners swarmed to the platform with compliments and handshakes.

One of them was Thornton Haggis, who had been given credit in the printed program for his historical research. He said, "Qwill, you slick operator! You really brought my dead notes to life!"

"Come to the barn for a celebration one day this week," Qwilleran said.

As he was packing his gear, Gary rushed

into the so-called dressing room with a cordless phone. "A call for you, Qwill. She says it's urgent."

Susan Exbridge was on the line, without her usual flip manner. "Qwill! Could you come to the dedication at Mount Vernon as soon as possible? Something awful has happened! I need to talk to you."

"Where'll I find you? Is there a large crowd?"

"Not too many. I'll watch for you driving down the Parkway and be out in front. You can pick me up. Then we can talk in private."

Mystified by the call, he asked Maxine to finish packing the gear, and he left the hotel by a back door.

Chapter Fifteen

The dedication of the Carroll Memorial Museum had not been planned as a public spectacle; it was more of a symbolic ceremony and news event. When Qwilleran arrived in answer to Susan Exbridge's urgent call, he found cars parked on both sides of the Parkway, including photographers' vans and the airport limousine rented by the TV crew from Down Below, but there were few persons in sight. They were indoors, as he later learned. But Susan was on the sidewalk in front of the building, ready to flag down Qwilleran's SUV.

When he pulled up, she opened the door and jumped in. "Park over there," she said.

"Where's Edythe? Is she all right?"

"For publication . . . she's all right. In the ceremony on the portico she handed over the key to the mayor and accepted an armful of roses, and a clergyman said a blessing, and now they're indoors — with officers of the historical society — having tea, but when it's over and I take her home . . . I'll need your advice, Qwill."

"You'll have to fill me in. Wait until I park properly."

He found a spot from which they could see the dignitaries leaving the building, and his hand went briefly into his jacket pocket as Susan began to talk.

"Well, to begin with . . . Edythe has always avoided the glare of publicity, and her husband shielded her from it. They had fifty beautiful years together — Dr. Dell and the ballerina! It was a real romance. Knowing this, I was sure she'd be nervous before the dedication, so I offered to stay with her. We had dinner last night in the residents' dining room, and I spent the night on a rather uncomfortable daybed in the spare room where she has her weaving loom and Dr. Dell's stationary bicycle, which she can't bear to part with.

"This morning we were having a pleasant continental breakfast in the apartment, when the reception desk in the lobby called and said that someone claiming to be Mrs. Carroll's granddaughter was there, and would it be all right to send her upstairs?

"Edythe gave the okay but looked worried. She said, 'What could I do? She's my own flesh and blood.' Older people around here are always talking about flesh and blood as an excuse for anybody doing anything. I hate that expression. But the doorbell rang, and there stood Edythe's flesh and blood, looking like a hobo and carrying a shabby duffel bag. Edythe gave her a grandmotherly hug that didn't seem genuine, and asked how she got here.

"Alicia said, 'I hitched a ride. I was tired of camping out. I want to stay here. I'll sleep on the floor if you don't have a bed.' Edythe showed her to the spare room and the shower, and gave her some towels.

"After a shower and change of clothes, the young woman still looked like a hobo, and I was sure she'd attend the dedication and embarrass her grandmother.

"Alicia said, 'No, I'll just stay here and pedal Gramps's bike and cry — while you're giving away my inheritance to this dump of a town.'

"Edythe said, 'You don't need a six-bedroom house; you'll have two trust funds and other property.' I found it appalling and excused myself, saying I'd be back at two o'clock to take her to the dedication. I had customers in the building who had heirloom furniture to sell. When I returned, Edythe was dressed and ready to go — wearing her lavender silk that looks so good with her silvery gray hair and alabaster complexion. To my shocked surprise, her face looked gray and drawn. No wonder! Alicia had just concocted a horrendous lie — that Dr. Dell had abused her while she was in high school, and that's why she left right after graduation.

"It was so untrue, Qwill, but that wicked girl knew how to hurt her grandmother. No intelligent person in Brrr would believe it, but there are always malicious gossips who enjoy spreading nasty rumors."

He turned off the tape recorder and said doubtfully, "Is there anything at all I can do? I certainly feel bad about it."

"Yes! Would you come home with us after the dedication? Supposedly to have a cup of tea, but really because you're an important person, and your presence might do some good. Edythe isn't asking this, I'm asking this."

Qwilleran "shifted gears," as he liked to say. He became an important person instead of a somewhat tired actor. "Let's go indoors here and shake some hands!" Hand shaking was part of his job at the *Moose County Something*.

Everyone in the drawing room was well dressed, and Qwilleran was wearing rehearsal clothes, but there were no rules for important persons. Casually he let it be known that he had just come from doing a matinee of the Great Storm show. Everyone had heard that it was wonderful.

A dozen persons were standing about the drawing room, holding teacups, when he strode into the room. There were gasps! They recognized the moustache of the author of the "Qwill Pen" column.

First he clasped Edythe's right hand in two of his, said she looked lovely, and complimented her on her magnificent gesture in donating a historic treasure to the community. No town could be more deserving!

He shook hands with the mayor, a hearty fellow with a grip like a vise, who said, "You should have made the speech — it would have been a heck of a lot better than mine!"

He shook hands with the pastor, who said, "My wife and I take turns reading your column aloud — she on Tuesday, me on Friday!"

He shook hands with the president of the local historical society, who begged him to speak at one of their meetings.

He even drank a cup of tea!

When it was over, he offered his arm and asked, "May I escort you to Ittibittiwassee, where all the best people live? That color you're wearing looks especially good on you."

"Thank you," she said. "Lavender is my birthday color — November, you know."

"Do you also have a birthday poem?"

"I never did until you wrote about the idea in your column. Now I'm going to adopt my husband's favorite poem — Shakespeare's thirtieth sonnet. Dell loved the last two lines!"

In the lobby of Ittibittiwassee Estates, he was hailed on all sides, thus adding to his acclaim as an important person.

When they arrived at the door of suite 400, Edythe gave him her keys. He unlocked it and pushed the door gently open. She walked in, and her knees buckled. Qwilleran caught her. Her face, which had regained its alabaster look at the dedication, turned gray again.

"Call the infirmary! Quick!" he said.

Medics arrived with a stretcher.

"I'll go with her," Susan said.

"Do you think I have her permission to call the police?"

"Absolutely!"

Only then did Qwilleran have time to assess the damage. The glass doors of the china cabinet were open, and all the miniature shoes — four shelves full — were gone. The only one remaining was on the floor, smashed.

Only the Meissen shoe on the bedside table was undisturbed.

Elsewhere, Qwilleran found Lish's grungy duffel bag in a wastebasket. A closet door stood open, showing several small pieces of designer luggage, but no large fortnighter. That had been used to transport the loot . . . with towels? There were none in the bathroom and few in the linen closet. The porcelains could be layered between thicknesses of terry cloth.

Susan returned to the apartment. "The cardiologist is there. Are the police coming?"

"The sheriff is sending a deputy. He or she will want to know the number and value of the objects stolen."

Susan said, "There's a ledger in the desk drawer. Dr. Dell kept meticulous records. Edythe once told me it was almost ten thousand, and that was before inflation."

Qwilleran said he'd stay until after the deputy's visit. Susan said Dr. MacKenzie had ordered an ambulance from the hospital.

Qwilleran drove home via Indian Village to ensure that Polly had not drowned. She had just arrived, quite dry.

"I see you didn't fall in," he said. "How was it?"

"The boat ride was lovely, if you like boats. The company was congenial. The picnic lunch was superb. Janice gave me some crabmeat Roquefort sandwiches to take home. No crust. I don't know whether you like that sort of tea-party fare."

"Ask me!"

"We can have some celery sticks and iced tea and sit on the deck."

He would have preferred iced coffee, but on a Fourth of July weekend, iced tea seemed more patriotic.

"Excuse me while I change into something comfortable."

"Do you mind if I tune in the six-o'clock news?"

There were soccer scores . . . and a barn fire on Sandpit Road . . . and a fatal accident on Bixby Highway, south of the county line. A young woman driving south crossed the yellow line into the northbound lane and plowed head-on into the Bixby Airport bus. The victim had not been identified, but she was driving an out-of-state vehicle.

Polly came down the stairs from the balcony. "Did you hear that?" she demanded. "You'd expect that of an older woman having a heart attack."

"She was calling her boyfriend on the cell phone," Qwilleran said.

"Did your show go well today?"

"I wowed 'em! I'll get you a ticket for next Sunday afternoon."

"Did you attend the dedication, dear?"

"I was late for the presentation of the key, but I got there in time for the tea indoors. The cookies weren't very good."

There was more, but Qwilleran had to go home and feed the cats.

When Qwilleran drove into the barnyard, a furry blur in the kitchen window indicated that dinner was late. Both Koko and Yum Yum took supervisory posts on top of the bar while he arranged their food attractively on two plates, one serving larger than the other. In the midst of the chore the phone rang, and Qwilleran grabbed the handset on the wall, expecting a report from Susan.

It was Gary Pratt. "Qwill! Did you hear the six-o'clock news? Fatal accident on Bixby Highway. It was Lish Carroll!"

"How do you know?"

"A deputy I went to high school with came into the bar. We both knew her and thought she was a character."

"How come she was driving? I thought she'd been denied a license."

"Who knows? Nobody's been able to figure her out since ninth grade. Well, I've got to get back to work. Thought you'd like to have the inside dirt."

Qwilleran's first reaction was: What happened to the porcelain shoes?

His second reaction was to phone Susan and tip her off about the accident. Edythe's doctor might want to censor the news from reaching her bedside.

Susan had just arrived home from the hospital — exhausted. "I've been playing big sister to Edythe for twenty-four hours. I'll call Dr. MacKenzie at once, about this new development. He calls her a brave woman. He wants her in the hospital for a week for observation. Edythe doesn't mind; she says he's charming. And he happens to be a widower."

With that mission completed, Qwilleran fed the cats and prepared to satisfy his own ravenous hunger resulting from an emotional performance onstage. He started heating some beef barley soup from the deli and building a heroic ham sandwich on rye augmented by an equally heroic dill pickle.

He had no sooner turned off the burner under the soup than Koko staged a first-class tizzy. He hopped on and off the kitchen counter, pressing his nose against the window screen that overlooked the approach to the barnyard. Something important was arriving. The cat was perturbed enough to suggest that it was a fire truck or an army tank.

Qwilleran went outdoors to investigate, first covering the soup pot and hiding the sandwich in a cat-proof cabinet. When a vehicle came through the woods, one could always hear the motor and crunching of tires on crushed stone. There was none of that, but a lone walker came into view, trudging wearily through the woods. He was wearing boots, skinny jeans, a loose hip-length jacket, and shoulder-length hair. He was the remaining half of the Lish-and-Lush team.

Chapter Sixteen

Qwilleran went to meet the weary traveler. "Clarence! Where did you come from?"

"The camp," the young man gasped, as if with his last breath.

"Great Oaks? That's ten miles from here! I hope you were able to hitch a ride." It was not likely; local drivers were not prone to pick up hitchhikers with haircuts different from their own.

"Have you had food, Clarence?"

The young man shook his head. "Couldn't pay for any. She's gone. Didn't leave no money."

"Well, come into the gazebo and have a bowl of soup and a ham sandwich." He showed Clarence to a lounge chair. "Stretch out here. Take off your boots. Munch on these nuts while you're waiting. Would you like some fruit juice?"

"Any beer?"

"Sorry. No beer." There was beer — and

everything else — in the bar, but Qwilleran preferred to keep the party dry.

In the barn he gave the soup another shot of heat and slipped another slice of ham into the sandwich. The cats watched — Yum Yum bemused, Koko mystified; the male cat always wanted to know the who, why, and what. Qwilleran was wondering how to break the news of the car accident. Lish was simply "gone," as far as her driver knew . . . and how indeed could he hold a conversation with this man of few words?

Back in the gazebo the guest wolfed down the repast that the host had intended for himself, but that was simply one of the quiddities in the life of the Klingenschoen heir.

Qwilleran kept the questions casual. "How long have you worked for Lish?"

After a pause, "I dunno."

"It's hard to remember, isn't it? Time flies. Did she leave you a note?"

He shook his head while chewing.

"Do you have any idea where she would go?"

"Nope."

"Where's your own home, may I ask? If I'm not being too nosy."

"Don't have none."

"Do you just hang out?"

He nodded.

"Yes. I guess young people like that life-style," Qwilleran added, trying not to sound too judgmental.

"Lish is a smart woman. She said you were a good driver. Do you like your work?"

Another nod.

"What other jobs do you do for her?"

"I'm her shooter." He said it with pride, it seemed.

"You mean, with a camera? Is she into photography?"

For an answer, the "shooter" opened his loose jacket and showed something shiny in a holster, close to his rib cage.

"Neat!" Qwilleran commented, for want of a better reaction.

He pondered the next question. "How about a dish of ice cream, and I'll have one, too. Would you like chocolate sauce?" The host brought two dishes, saying genially, "Nothing like a big dish of ice cream at the end of a hard day. Now tell me about your shooting. It must be interesting."

"I only did it twice."

"Do you remember where?"

"Once down on the beach, somewhere around here, and once up north."

"Who were the guys? Do you know?"

The answer was a shrug.

"I hope your boss was pleased with your work. I suppose you came back up here for the celebration."

"Nah. She was mad at her grandma. I thought she'd want another shootin', but she didn't."

Qwilleran thought, This could be a comedy turn, if it weren't so tragic. "What will you do now that she's taken the car?"

"She'll come back."

"I don't think so, Clarence. She had an accident this afternoon. It was on the radio. She was killed."

The young man stared.

"Did you hear me? She was killed — instantly — and the car was smashed."

With what seemed like regret, Clarence said, "And I always kept it so clean!"

The fellow's remark struck Qwilleran as revealing. The boss was dead, the car was totaled, and he was grieving over the polish he kept on it. There was the look in his eyes, the dilation of his pupils that indicated he was "messed up" on drugs. Qwilleran had once been "messed up," but on alcohol — homeless, penniless, jobless, and friendless. Then strangers had snatched him back from the Valley of Death — literally. And the incident had turned him around. But he had not murdered anyone; Clarence had shot that man down on the beach. Lish had staged the event, finding the victim and possibly disappearing with the loot. All that was canceled out by her head-on collision with the Bixby Airport bus, leaving Clarence to face the music. Whether he was high on crack or simply dull-witted, the situation was the same: He had been the shooter, and he was in trouble.

Qwilleran asked, "What will you do now that Lish is gone? You were the shooter, and you'll have to take the blame for the murders. Do you realize you'll be arrested, put on trial, sent to prison?"

The black pupils that passed for eyes in the pathetic face darted back and forth.

"I'll phone my lawyer. He'll do the best he can for you. I'll have to go inside to get his number and try to track him down. I'll send my friend Koko out to keep you company. Do you like cats?"

He nodded without enthusiasm.

Qwilleran returned with the cat in his tote bag, tipping him out gently on the table at Clarence's elbow. The two were regarding each other questioningly as Qwilleran hurried back into the barn.

First he did his civic duty by calling Andrew Brodie. The police chief was always at home, watching TV, on Sunday evenings. "Andy, police news! The man who shot the victim on my beach property is in my gazebo, playing with Koko. He's a sad sack, and I feel bad about turning him in. I think his partner has kept him in a drugged state to make him follow orders. His partner was killed in that airport-bus crash."

Qwilleran froze as he heard a gunshot! "Oh, my God! Has he shot Koko?"

Dropping the phone with a crash, Qwilleran rushed out to the gazebo . . . There was the cat, standing on the table, arching his back to twice its usual height, and bushing his tail to four times its usual size. In the chair slumped Clarence, with blood running from a bullet hole in his temple.

Qwilleran ran back to the phone. He spluttered, "Andy . . . Andy. There's a new development —"

"Be right there! Don't let him get away!" the chief said.

"He's not going anywhere. Bring the body wagon," Qwilleran shouted.

Chapter Seventeen

 The gossips had little grist for their mill. As always, local police and news media respected Qwilleran's desire for anonymity. The perpetrators of the homicide were dead, and Koko, the only witness to the suicide, was not talking. Edythe Carroll was back in her Ittibittiwassee apartment under the close supervision of Dr. Mac-Kenzie, along with her collection of miniature porcelain shoes. They had survived the collision, thanks to the sturdiness of the luggage, the way it was lodged in the back of the car, and the thickness of the bath towels.

These developments left Qwilleran gratefully free to concentrate on the "Qwill Pen" column and the "Great Storm" show, which was playing twice weekly to full houses. Polly Duncan and the Rikers attended the second matinee, after which they met for a picnic in the gazebo: drinks courtesy of Arch, casserole by Mildred, celery sticks and low-calorie dessert by Polly.

"How come this place looks so clean?" asked Arch Riker, a master of the brutal compliment.

"The cats spend a lot of time out here, and they shed. It's about time I had it cleaned."

The truth was that the fussy pair had boycotted the gazebo ever since the gunshot and would not return until the cleaning crew had scoured everything and left a comforting aroma of detergent.

The party of four plunged into the refreshments and the conversation — lauding Qwilleran for his performance, Maxine for her composure, Mrs. Carroll for her munificence, and the town of Brrr for its spunky birthday party.

Mildred asked, "Who on earth would think of that crazy birthday cake stunt?"

"Gary Pratt. He's a nut," Arch said. "Why does he go around looking like a bear?"

"Because he's president of the chamber of commerce," Qwilleran said, "and this is Moose County, and he can look any way he wants!"

"Your set!" Arch conceded, having watched the tennis matches on television. "Let's talk about the bookstore. How's it coming?"

Polly had been waiting politely to be asked. "We've hired a bibliocat — a handsome marmalade with magic green eyes — and we're looking at carpet samples to match them. Also, we've lined up a former teacher from the Lockmaster Academy of the Arts who'll work part-time."

"What's his name?" asked Mildred, who prided herself on knowing everyone.

"Alden Wade. The cat's name is Dundee. I have a snapshot of him in my handbag. Would you like to see it?"

"The teacher or the cat?" Arch asked.

"My husband is being arch," Mildred said.

Dundee's cream-and-apricot markings and alert appearance and fascinating eyes were admired.

Then Arch said, "Qwill, I can't resist asking any longer. What's that thing on the side table?" He pointed to a small block of wood and a paddle.

"A turkey call," Qwilleran explained. "The Outdoor Club was selling them to raise money for a good cause, so I bought a few to give to friends who hunt game birds. I use this one to tease Koko. He talks back to it. He thinks he can talk turkey."

"Now I've heard it all! Let's go home."

The guests carried the dishes into the barn, and the women tidied the kitchen while Qwilleran fed the cats. Arch had learned that he could be most helpful by keeping out of the way, so he wandered around and made comments:

"I see you've got a new phone. . . . Who made this turned wood gadget with paper clips in it? . . . I see Koko knocked an Uncle Wiggily book off the shelf. . . . Are you still reading to the cats?"

The guests drove away, and Qwilleran transported the cats to the gazebo in their tote bag, along with a book about a rabbit who wore a top hat and had gentlemanly manners. Yum Yum had smuggled her silver thimble to the gazebo in the tote bag and proceeded to bat it around the concrete floor. Koko was sitting on his brisket near the screen, as if waiting for something to happen.

"Are you waiting for the mailman?" Qwilleran asked. "Waiting for Santa Claus? Waiting for Godot?"

The cat turned and regarded him pityingly — or so it seemed.

Suddenly Qwilleran felt weary, not only from the effort of doing a one-man show and the excitement of partying afterward, but also from the whole Lish-and-Lush experience, climaxed by the suicide in his own backyard. He felt the urge to relax, do nothing, enjoy the early summer evening, give his vocal cords a hiatus. Perhaps he dozed off. Possibly he dreamed. He may have heard Koko clucking and gobbling.

He was sure he heard a rustling in the shrubbery, as two wild turkeys appeared, followed by a veritable horde of poults — all the same size. More large birds with red wattles came from the back road, saw the barn, and put their heads together as if critiquing the architecture.

Had Koko invited them? Was this why he had been waiting and watching?

Even as Qwilleran stared at the scene, the congregation began to drift away into the bushes. The last to leave were the poults, with lingering glances back at Koko, perhaps wishing they could have stayed longer.

A high-decibel yowl directly in his ear catapulted Qwilleran out of his lounge chair. Koko was on the chairside table.

"You devil!" he shouted.

Koko nudged the volume of Uncle Wiggily stories.

Qwilleran obliged — reading the honorable doings of Uncle Wiggily. The cat had lost interest in "The Shooting of Dan

McGrew" and *The Hunting of the Snark*, but — it might be noted — not until Lish and Lush had been identified with the two "woodland murders."

Simmons, who thought "snark" sounded like something spelled backwards, would be amused to know that it spelled KRANS. . . . "Kranson" was the real surname of Alicia and her felonious parent.

Qwilleran had to admit that the connection was preposterous; it was purely coincidental. . . . But what about Koko's reactions to Lish from the very beginning? He had growled at her when she walked down the beach; he had hissed at her message on the phone! All cats have a sense of right and wrong, but Koko's clairvoyance was beyond belief! There was one incontrovertible fact, and that was the authenticity of his blood-curdling death howl signifying wrongful death. It could be a mile away or a continent away, but it was always connected with an individual or a situation close to home.

"Yow!" said Koko, on the table at Qwilleran's elbow and staring with a fathomless gaze, after which he rolled over onto his spine and attended to a sudden catly itch.

"Not on the table!" came the scolding,

but Kao K'o Kung went on doing what had to be done.

"N-n-now!" came a delicate cry from Yum Yum. With the silver thimble clamped in her little jaws, she jumped to Qwilleran's lap and gave him her favorite toy.

About the Author

Lilian Jackson Braun is the author of twenty-six Cat Who novels and three short story collections.